*The*

# CURE

## KEN PETERS

*Dedication*

*To Sloane, who left us all too soon. Your life and your love will endure for all of your family and friends forever*

# ACKNOWLEDGMENTS

*Many thanks to all who have been in the fight to find a vaccine for HIV. For the extensive publications, papers and abstracts by many HIV researchers including by Dr. Anthony Fauci, Dr. Richard Besser and other virologists located in Johannesburg South Africa at the National Institute of Communicable Diseases whose concepts on facets of the HIV disease transmission formed the basis of this story's concept. To all of those I worked with for four years in Cape Town, South Africa; Patricia Richards, Lynette Rooiland, Anwar Bull and many more than can be named herein who educated me on customs, culture and the HIV Pandemic. Frank Fadil whose creativity brought me the cover for this book. I'd also like to thank a nameless family for privacy reasons in Uganda, where I spent time gathering further research on the HIV crisis in Africa. The last and most important tribute is my acknowledgment to Joy Brown, who always encouraged me to get back to work and refers to me as her Hemingway, as all authors always require encouragement to complete their work when life creates roadblocks.*

© Ken Peters 2021

ISBN: 978-1-09835-184-7

eBook ISBN: 978-1-09835-185-4

This is a work of fiction. Characters, corporations, institutions, and organizations in this novel are either the product of the author's imagination or, if real are used as public institutions in a fictitious manner without any intent to describe their actual conduct.

# PREFACE

Three hundred years ago, at the turn of the 18th century, Africa was the jewel of the British, French, Portuguese, Dutch and Spanish Empires with established colonies. Those colonies provided valuable resources and routes of trade. The winds of time, however, brought growth, political change, wars, and liberalism that caused colonialism to fade slowly, as the moon wanes if watched day by day. It was ever unnoticeable, yet ever changing at its own tempo as the centuries passed.

The rising new world orders brought conflicts to every corner of the globe. The Muslim fanatics were revolting in the Middle East and terror was spreading from S.E. Asia to the Urals of the former Soviet Union and beyond. Despite this encroaching global war of cultures, the rich syndicates, cadres, industrialists or the old established families of Western Europe, by whatever name one chooses to define the powerful, for them such turmoil in the developing nations only meant opportunities amid the chaos.

The growth of these oligarchs and their business holdings went unnoticed by the major world powers. The world of politics had different goals. The seizing of international resources was accomplished through the vehicle of political ideology. It operated in a world largely ignorant of the ideological underpinnings derived from their former colonial holdings. Such was the economic power residing in the private corners of Vienna, the Netherlands, Germany or Switzerland.

However, profit in the new 21st century was marked more by scrutinizing the constantly shifting shares and acquisitions of powerful economic conglomerates. Large multinational corporations were being watched—and exposed by the new world press. MSNBC, CNN and even Al-Jazeera all had their own competitive economic agendas vying for profits and ratings. But while the press held court via satellite networks, in the dark clandestine corners of the private elite clubs of old Europe, secret meetings were being held with a completely different agenda by the former colonial families of Africa.

Inside the inner sanctums of these old world fortunes that still controlled huge economic power, often hidden behind Swiss bank accounts, a new world order was taking shape. These small clandestine cadres of power were implicitly receiving assistance for their own agendas as emerging third world nations were devolving. The so called budding democratic governments were being scrutinized with screams of foul play in the world press, as contracts for arms, infrastructure and other major capital expenditures were being made by despots operating under the guise of democracy while the real wealth only went to the privileged.

The Dark Continent, Africa, as it always had been known before, was laid rich with natural resources and minerals. The reach of these former colonial Robber Barons was beyond calculation via secret holdings and could remain unnoticed while the radical specter of terrorism was being fought by Democracies of the first world. A new world order would be coming to Africa, but no one could have predicted it would be from its former proprietors.

Africa stood alone and somewhat removed from the first world fight on terrorism due to its implicit poverty and the theft by its new leaders. The leaders of these former colonies had been in power for 40 years or more since their independence, but aid from the West continued unabated. They had a vested interest in maintaining the status quo, only to be turned over for vital strategic, geographic interest or the ten ton the elephant in the room, *oil!* Beyond that Africa was relegated to the bleeding liberals seeking to alleviate their western guilt.

However, but for the aforementioned, until AIDS became epidemic, Africa was almost unnoticed. Only the NGOs, faith-based charities and the liberal Media establishment of the 21st century, seeking to save the continent's people from their own morally and culturally bankrupt societies, took notice of Africa's plight. Recent population migrations to the continent's larger cities like Johannesburg, Lagos, Accra, Kinshasa, and Kigali did not go smoothly with traditional African culture clashing with the concept of modern cities.

Governments did not prepare for the population influx, nor were they inclined to deal with their own poor. Most of those arriving in the cities had before only lived in their distinct tribes where population was limited by what the land could provide in addition to war, disease and pestilence. Now as cities grew in Africa and the populations shifted, AIDS was ravaging country after country, while corrupt governments continued to steal the wealth of these nations.

The resources of the continent remains, just waiting to be harvested amidst the vacuum created by the corrupt governments. Despite all of the previous aid from the World Bank, IMF, other multilateral financial aid agencies, the withering population from AIDS made Africa ripe for the taking.

In recent times the disease of HIV was accelerating. AIDS consumed thousands of lives daily, only increasing geometrically due to primitive mores brought from a thousand years ago to modern day African cities. Indigenous customs where men of great physical prowess sired children to the best women of their tribe belonged to a time long ago, when men measured wealth by the number of offspring! However, the 21st century no longer belonged to small villages but to the growing cities where such sexual promiscuity no longer had a place. In this new urban world, where this disease runs rampant, society gives little moral value to concepts that might slow the spread, like abstinence.

Governments fought amongst themselves to access the donation spoils flooding in from liberal westerners of conscience seeking to morally change all of the wrongs wrought by centuries of colonialism. With the few wealthy becoming wealthier and the poor becoming poorer, there could never be a middle class, and hence there could never be any real chance for a democracy.

All of this was exacerbated by the technological information revolution. Now the African masses were subjected to consumerism of the first world, with the new and alluring lifestyles brought to them via the internet, television and satellite dishes. Western intervention into these still tribal and primitive cultures of Africa offered greater freedoms, but without a foundation to understand the consequences of misusing those freedoms. Viable roads enhanced transportation, bringing he rural to urban centers for employment. Though the tribal man had been brought to the 21st century, traditional tribal mindsets were antithetical to AIDS virus.

The reality, while barely acknowledged by most African leaders, was that by early 2004 between 30 to 55% of the African population was already infected with the HIV virus. By 2015 the multitudes of cheap labor would be eradicated. In the wake of such a depletion, Africa would once again be owned by their former landlords. Their descendants would use their family's wealth to retake what once belonged to their forefathers centuries ago. Amongst these clandestine wealthy inner circles, one might almost hear them whisper, "Bring them gifts of technology and lifestyle but keep them out of reach." Avarice and desire will lead to pandemonium and disorder and AIDS will bring us back that which was once our birthright!"

These technological advances, along with AIDS were now devastating the continent. The only solution to the AIDS crisis as seen by the democracies of the west was a vaccine; a panacea, one that could stem the tide in the fight against AIDS and save this continent. This vaccine, "The Cure," was discovered by a biotech group in Johannesburg in early

2007 but was kept secret to quell any expectations of success. The western nations had been seeking just such a solution! But was this vaccine, now hidden in a deep vault in a small unknown biotech company, the answer to save the continent?

TRANSGENE Biotech of South Africa was a private, small company funded through multilateral public health organizations, as well as by investments from major pharmaceutical companies worldwide, hoping to share in the profits of a successful vaccine. They had just completed three years of clinical trials. It was 2010 and they were ready to announce to the world the CURE had been successfully engineered.

# CHAPTER 1
# *A Morning's Business*

Small, descriptive advertisements were placed worldwide in industry trade journals. T The talents and skills sought were plentiful. What was not plentiful, however, were the secret criteria.

There would be no shortfall of applicants. The grueling interviews would take months. The criteria they sought was beyond ability, it was about background and personal information. Those who would fill these positions would need to be single and without ties or family. They would need the appearance of still participating in society, while in reality, having long since left the ranks of those with dreams of a future.

The genesis of this advertisement began with a clandestine group of six powerful men. Their motivations were similar, but disagreements remained on the means to justify the ends. They were the old world intellectual patriarchs of Europe. Their power resided in the ability to secretively coerce governments through vast wealth. Today, late in the first decade of the 21st century, they were the leaders of families who had for more than two centuries controlled massive amounts of money in Switzerland, Germany, Belgium, France, the Netherlands and the UK.

Their current net worth was derived from their fathers and grandfathers before them who seized it during the 19th century when the industrial revolution of the west enabled Europeans to accelerate seizure and settlement of African wealth.

At the meeting today was Nigel Jones age 75 and Roger Atwell age 77, two men who had once controlled more than 85% of the exports and imports to Zimbabwe. The country, formerly Rhodesia, was once the breadbasket of Africa. The men had been business partners for almost a half a century.

Almost like a Dickens novel, they lived their lives around the wealth they had accumulated yet took little pleasure from it beyond the old world estate surrounding their daily comportment. They indulged not thoughts toward using their wealth to enjoy life. One might think that such men believed they would live forever! They both resided in west England's Exmore country on grand estates, insulated from the common, but with all the technology to operate their empires without traveling.

Neither man could count any of their children or grandchildren worthy to fill their shoes in regards to taking over their respective empires. The two of them, as time had gone by, kept increasingly to themselves. Even family members needed clearance from their respective servants to get into the house. Their world view was shrinking, becoming more about what they confided to each other.

More and more their discussions centered upon what must be done to preserve their respective empires. For surely if nothing was done in the next 25 years, their families would lose their vast power. Money was important, but power established control. Patricians were never satisfied with money, power was the ultimate wealth!

Post the world's financial debacle of 2008, the wealthiest worldwide were under a new scrutiny as wealth distribution became consolidated. A reset button was going to be pushed, and many things were going to change. The future of their families had to be secured,, even if none of their descendants were deserving of their wealth. The name must be maintained.

But their wealth would have to be removed from Europe where the EU was devolving into turmoil. Both Nigel and Roger kept this goal and their friendship foremost in their minds. They had been school mates since primary school. Their families had been very close, and Roger and Nigel were as close as brothers. Their family estates in Yorkshire abutted one another and so through the years whether riding or involved with pranking local farmers, they were thick as thieves.

After graduation, Nigel spent some time as a Chartered accountant while Roger became a solicitor working in his family's law firm, Atwell, Hackett and Lawton. After a few years Nigel was sent to Africa to oversee several of the family's interests. He continued to rise in responsibilities until by age 50 he was granted the position of managing director for his family's interests in their own conglomerate of companies known as Thames Commodity Brokerage. By that time the law firm owned by Roger's family had long since been partnered with Thames Commodity Brokerage and it was but a short jump for Nigel and Roger as old friends to begin melding much of the investments and fortunes to work jointly.

Another of the group, Fritz Kronner, was an 82-year- old of Swiss man whose family holdings accounted for more than twenty two different banks found in Uganda, Kenya, Zambia (northern Rhodesia), Namibia (former SW South Africa) and the Republic of South Africa. Fritz's family emigrated to SW Africa in the 1820's. His great grandfather and his two brothers all were educated in Berne and had attained degrees well suited for exploration into Africa.

As young lads the three brothers, a geologist, an engineer and an architect set out for adventure and fortune. Arriving in SW Africa their skills were in high demand and they quickly found their legs and began the family's Africa Empire. From there it was a straight path into the world of mining given, their critical usefulness in analyzing underground conditions. Their efforts avoided dangerous rock formations which might not support tunnels for the mining of gold, diamonds and copper.

Given the European rush toward Africa and the lure of great wealth through gold, it wasn't long after that the Kronner brothers began banking on a small scale by lending money to stake holders who were undercapitalized. This usually led to seizing their properties based on defaults. Banking became just another route to continue to control more and more of the land and mines. It became a spinoff business which generated funds to be moved back to Switzerland and fuel their Swiss banks.

Next was Roger Atwell, 69 years old of Belgium. His family formerly ran the railroads and the infrastructure at the port city of Boma in the Belgium Congo. They were early facilitators for the ships coming in from Europe, distributing incoming good as and sending materials back. The Atwell family built many of the European railroads and as Africa became more and more colonized with the advent of trade, the Atwell family saw the value of building miles and miles of train infrastructure as demand for goods was dire from surrounding countries. As the resources surrounding the port city diminished, the family pushed further into the interior, seeking untouched reserves yet to be harvested by the thriving colonists.

The family of Franz Heren, age 79, had once controlled most of the farming enterprises in South Africa. His family had immigrated to in the 1680's to the Western Cape and from there the family's fortunes expanded exponentially in those early days. It stretched as far north as Vintners. Their dairy holdings extended as far as Zimbabwe, into the Rift valley from Caper Town.

Lastly among the Group of six was Fredrich Dressel, age 86. For more than his seniority, the chair of this private and exclusive group. His family's wealth wasn't derived from the old world but out of Nazi Germany's once huge fortunes, stolen and transferred in art, gold and other treasures during WWII.

Dressel was a former SS Colonel who oversaw Hitler's art treasuries. Starting in 1945, those assets were secreted out of Europe and sent to South Africa. His family had settled in there after the Boer war and became major political leaders, founding the Nationalist party and beginning Apartheid. His roots of self-righteousness and criminality were well developed through the SS.

Fredrich was a self-made man, if only through theft, but nevertheless the wealth he stole was the wealth he brought to South Africa. It built his empire by financing the support of Nationalist party politicians who in return, after election, granted huge portions of prime real estate upon which the foundations of the great city of Johannesburg were built. His wealth continued to grow while building vast shopping centers and becoming one of if not the largest commercial developer in South Africa. Eventually, after the change of government, he had to relinquish, due to the new government of black rule, a 51% share of all his enterprises to the indigenous stake holders of that country.

Each of the group of six had to turn much of their family's fortunes over to indigenous quasi businessmen in recent decades. These recipients, using the political system, took control of the former white European built businesses. In essence, the leaders of these new African governments used the independence movements to seize businesses for their own benefit. For the people, in some instances more than four decades had gone by and instead of democracy and growth, only dictatorships under the guise of democracy evolved, and the poor remained impoverished.

Of course, independence and anti-colonial movements were always done in the name of the people, but nevertheless those indigenous people who seized political power always seized the wealth. This same scenario repeated across numerous African nations as they won independence in the latter part of the 20th century.

The concept of retaking the continent, which was once theirs and their families alone, by removing all such indigenous impediments, was not even remotely considered wrong or immoral, particularly by Fredrich Dressler.

By any means, it was justified to retake that which was stolen from them during the decolonization in the name of independence. With great ire, for the group of 6 this was the ultimate affront and insult to have Being forced to provide a minimum of a 51% share ownership of their assets for no capital and with no effort was a great affront to these six men. They gave it up for no other reason than corrupt reverse racial concepts of these new rulers who took from what the colonists built for their own greed. The new black empowered entrepreneurs of Africa put little into anything, but seized all they could through reverse racism and justification of sovereignty. Front men in each country, who by law after independence, were given the rights and assets the continent at large.

With a plan at hand, the appropriate contacts were made by the Group of Six trading company. Adverts for recruitment had begun in worldwide new papers. The goal was to obtain maximum exposure to ensure they reached the right men to begin the first leg of their plan to retake what ultimately was theirs, and would belong to them again. There was to be no bias towards black, white, Indian or Asian. The task was merely to assess that they were retaining the very best in each field.

Since their plan required men to do that which was illicit, the main motivation for all those recruited was money. Their former lives had to display a certain amount of upheaval, either through their own fault or through the shifting fortunes of economies. Where possible, it was beneficial if their lives were now low profile or even off the grid and not traceable. It would be critical that no one would be brought in if they had any link to any other individuals on this mission. For the plan to be ultimately successful, no one could have had any previous contacts or know previously any of their cohorts.

The plot offered up to these recruits would be simple industrial espionage. The plan called for skills to address the following areas. First, a genetic engineer who could splice and change the formula for a vaccine. Second an individual to obtain access into a secure location. A location where the value of its secret assets well exceeded hundreds of millions of dollars.

To steal a revolutionary vaccine that was destined to change the face of the world would require overcoming the highest security hurdles. The plan would call for two individuals, a software engineer to create the secure passes to get through the electronic security, and a facilitator for movement. The skills needed would require breaking in without leaving a trace. This would require the best of hackers. Next would be a forward observer whose job it would be to monitor the break-in remotely of their target, the biotech facilities of Transgene. They would keep tabs on potential late employees and security personnel.

Last a logistics person was needed to make the arrival and departure seamless through all the various destinations and to eliminate any trace of their entry into the country. This would require someone who had worked and lived in the airline security business, allowing the group to travel like a shadow, leaving no trace with any airline or immigration entry point. Given the security issues of a post 911 world, this would require very special skills.

Most important to the plan was the master coordinator, the one doing the actual interviews, recruitment and background validations of those hired. That being accomplished, the team assembled would be ready, short of intensive training to ensure each knew their job. However there was the issue anonymity.

The Group of Six determined that the recruits would be given new identities and start a life anew with their compensation from this job. As noted, these were all men without families or ties and for then such new identities were a bonus. Each team member were given their new passports and understood that any breach of this project prior to commencement would cost 50% of their promised payment. Frankly the Group of Six was not concerned, for there were contingency plans for each member of the team should there ever be a violation of this project's secrecy.

The Group of Six had always seen all individuals involved in this affair as quite disposable should anything go awry. After all, the opera-

7

tives were single, with no family ties and implicit in their pursuit of the advertisement, they had nothing to lose and everything to gain. Their past lives no longer offered them anything. The compensation the Group of Six were offering was enough to take any man or woman off the legal grid forever.

# CHAPTER 2
# *The Plan Hatches*

It was 10:00 AM. The room was large with wooden panels hailing back 800 years to when this castle was first built. They were inlaid with ornate symbols recalling a time when Prussia was a part of Europe controlled by fiefdoms. The curtains were all drawn and a hearth, 6 feet in height was lit with a hearty fire to warm the ancient space.

Above the hearth hung an original Renoir painting. Set at each corner of a grand conference table were serving trays set with silver platters and china teacup sets. At the table were six chairs, tufted and upholstered in a deep burgundy. Their arms were carved wood with high backs topped with a crown.

The board room was set at a mezzanine level. Two stewards stood at attention as the men of the Group of Six each entered the vestibule hall. Their coats were taken and they were directed towards the grand stair case in the center of the formal hall.

They ascended to the mezzanine level. First was Nigel Jones, followed by Roger Atwell, then Franz Heren, Roger Collier, Frtiz Kronner and lastly Fredrich Dressler. Once inside the formidable board room, they each sat and casually greeted each other by head nods to the left and the right. Fredrich Dressler took the seat at the head of the table. Once tea was served, the stewards were asked to leave.

Fredrich wore a dark smile and spoke with a chilling tone. "Gentlemen thanks to one of our own, Nigel Jones, we are meeting to finalize the plan to retake our family's possessions. It is brilliant, and worthy of our assemblage."

He nodded to Nigel, who stood before the group and unfolded the details of their endeavor and its anticipated outcome. When he was done, Fredrick again took the floor.

"Gentlemen our candidates have been selected. Our team for our operation is complete. What remains now are the details of capital assets and implementation. Each actor has been secured with a $250,000 deposit in the bank of their choice. I am quite confident each of them will follow through in anticipation of their rewards to come. They all understand another $250,000 will be deposited into their accounts just prior to the mission's commencement, with the balance paid upon completion. That will be an additional $1,000,000. The total of 1.5 million is more than any of our recruits had ever hoped to earn in their lifetimes."

---

Although Fredrich was indeed the leader, as he had the least morals as might be expected from a former SS colonel, it was Nigel and Roger who were the active players. They developed the strategy. They were the real thinkers. In fact, it was Nigel in concert with Roger that brought the idea to fruition.

The Group of Six as a cadre backed the strategy to repatriate Africa's assets to the rightful owners, those who developed Africa. Initially in the 80s and& 90s they found it easy to accumulate what they believed theirs by buying off corrupt governments. Those in power were always consumed by greed. Although the price paid was ever increasing, it still seemed a viable path, even if it galled the Group of Six to be levered by those of lesser status. In any event, they had to come to accept the situation as their singular path to repatriate the assets of their heritage.

The new plan, funded by the Group was known as "The Cure." Its genesis came through happenstance. Nigel Jones had changed the fortunes of the Group of Six in a manner beyond their wildest dreams. Being highly educated at Eton, and a corporate accountant with both public and privately held firms, Nigel was privy to sensitive information. Through a Bond Street friend, he received regular inside information on a company called Transgene Biotech of South Africa and their progress toward certain infectious disease vaccines.

He began making significant investments in Transgene. So significant that he was given access to asymmetric non-public information. Despite Roger Atwell being one of Nigel's closest friends, greed being what it is, he hadn't at first told Roger about Transgene Biotech. However, as things were progressing , he brought Roger in to reap the potential benefits. Through his connections on Bond Street, Nigel was kept abreast of developments and was able to acquire further inside shares while company was still privately held. Being in tune with the 21st century biotechnology developments, he received word that Transgene Biotech had been working on a HIV vaccine, with completed clinical trials with excellent results. It had been submitted to the WHO (World Health Organization) in anticipation of bringing the vaccine to the market.

It was on a lovely summer evening at their private men's club in St. James, when Nigel revealed that Transgene had submitted to the WHO for the approval of its HIV vaccine. It was at this moment that their cognative tea kettle began brewing in an odd way. During the conversation they boasted to each other about the killing they'd make when the company went public.

Suddenly, Roger joked, "what if it doesn't work and all those inoculated died instead of being cured, wouldn't that be the Queen's justice"! He added an arrogant laugh, befitting an Englishman with a Patrician attitude for the less fortunate. But his chuckle did not have time to linger.

11

"Yes, wouldn't that be an interesting phenomenon…" Nigel mused. "What if it didn't work?"

"But if it's going to the WHO," Roger shot back. "the results must clearly show it to be a cure." a

Nigel's mind was turning. He proceeded to explain about how vaccines are made using live viruses, denaturing their DNA, and cloning a new DNA. But the new DNA would be engineered to be susceptible to an antibody that would fight and destroy the HIV virus.

Once the genetic code for the virus is broken, its nothing to reproduce antibodies at ridiculously low-cost levels. The expense of such a vaccine lies in the research, in the time and effort to sequence the genetics correctly for the vaccine. Then there are the trials, testing, and most important the evaluation of patient responses to statistically predict outcomes using predictive algorithms. It's all an extremely laborious effort. There are millions of genomes that need be worked through to achieve a successful vaccine.

Nigel sat up and stared. He met Roger's gaze with dead-serious eyes.

"Well if someone can alter a DNA sequence to make it kill the virus, can the concept be perverted to do the opposite? Sort of poisoning the well as it were." Nigel sat back and sipped his martini. "What if someone did alter the vaccine without anyone knowing it before it was released? Millions in fact would die and likely more than 50% of the African population would perish. Even more likely, the ridiculous leaders who are siphoning the coffers of these governments would be the first to get the vaccine."

## CHAPTER 3
## The Setup

Brian Smuts was contracted by a company jointly operated by the Group of Six known as Ziffer GMBH. Their primary business was banking for pharmaceutical and medical device companies doing business in third world countries requiring currency floats at very high interest rates. Ziffer was a good cover for the Group's illicit activities revolving around currency trading. Brian was not an employee but an independent contractor, to keep Ziffer at a further arm's length. His main territory was the continent of Africa. As such he worked with high government officials which also meant working with the *corrupt government officials*. After all, most of Africa was corrupt and the only ones getting rich were the elite and the governments they controlled.

As such Brian met many people of this ilk and some of even a lesser ilk, the bottom fishers of life and the lowest dealers on the continent. One of Brian's regular clients was the biotech company Genetic Resources Corporation (GRC). They sold research materials to governmental and private sectors, where delayed payments were commonplace. Ziffer being in touch with Brian Smuts was business as usual, as companies in South Africa were within his territory.

Ziffer's VP of finance, Geoffrey Wright, contacted Brian and asked him to come in for a confidential meeting regarding an issue with one of his regular clients. At the meeting Mr. Wright explained that one of their clients was involved in a project that they wanted Brian to head up. The ruse as presented had nothing to do with Ziffer, but rather was Ziffer simply trying to accommodate a client with a resource acquisition problem. Geoffrey Wright explained that Brian would be working for GRC.

This company was well known to him, and conversely Genetic Resources Corporation Ltd was familiar with Brian. A most amenable situation to do anything that was even slightly off the grid. They specialized in providing research materials to government and private laboratories for gene splicing, gels, agars, etc. Geoffrey explained that GRC had expressly asked for Brian to head up this project as they understood Brian had considerable knowledge of the bottom fishers of Africa.

It was at this meeting with Geoffrey Wright that Brian was informed that GRC had been working on a HIV vaccine which failed miserably after 3 years and a $250 million investment. Geoffrey kept the conversation convoluted to mask the industrial espionage project. Brian got the gist of what GRC was seeking, namely certain types of persons who have been involved in commercial espionage to steal a copy of the genetic code for the vaccine. Geoffrey Wright was emphatic such information was off the record and there was no recording of this conversation.

Brian's retainer was $500,000 and he would receive another $500,000 once the team was chosen, assembled and the project was completed. Being a logistics person, Brian was all too aware of the scope of this project. He was going to get a bit dirty recruiting the team and arranging to get the personnel in and out of Africa using non-commercial transport. Truly flying under the radar figuratively, and perhaps literally.

It was an offer Brian could not refuse, given he was only recruiting, coordinating and transporting the personnel, but not participating in anything that was actually illegal. Nothing was illegal about a plane flying under 300 feet in certain areas to avoid radar detection, however it might seem to South African Governmental Aviation authorities. In Africa it was common for air Safari's to fly low over herds of Water Buffalo, Zebra and Spring Boks.

To Brian Smuts at age 60, despite the understanding that something illegal was going to take place via his efforts, this could possibly be his last opportunity to score big. Although this presented a challenge, a $1,000,000 fee made no obstacle, legal or illegal, too great to overcome. Brian's life had become a less than a desirable one having lost his wife.

Brian had met his wife some twenty years before on a trip to England. As a man tired of loneliness from his constant travel and his native girlfriends who brought little to him other than servitude, he found great joy in meeting this nanny at a dinner party hosted by a Ziffer executive. He was outside having a cigarette at the end of the party when he met her. She too was taking a break with a cigarette and a conversation ensued. She was plenty tired of this indentured servitude working as a waitress during the day and catching odd jobs here or there in the evening for extra money as a server at the homes of wealthy Patricians in London.

Life for her in England, coming from a poor family, offered little for the future. When she came upon an advertisement seeking a nanny for a family in South Africa, it wasn't much of a leap to imagine this as a fantastic opportunity. Her imagination, fueled by movies like, "Out of Africa," was filled with romantic notions of an exciting new world to be discovered. For her it was life away from the dreary English weather and a hum-drum life working as a waitress in a breakfast shop. This worldly man, 20 years her senior intrigued her.

Brian, forty at the time, was heading back to Africa as a contract fixer, with a sizable income through contract fees. He presented to her a possible future of marriage and life in Africa. One far beyond the life she had been living as a waitress in England. Living in Africa meant an equal footing amongst other Europeans. It was a short jump from this encounter with Brian to a few dates with him in London to leap at his proposal despite only having known him for a few weeks.

When she first arrived in Africa, she was agog with life there for European whites. She experienced embassy and private parties with multinational executives from Heinz, P&G, Mobil Oil, etc. Servants did the laundry and house cleaning. It was truly a far superior life than she had back in England.

However, as life went on after arriving in Africa, Brian traveled ever more frequently throughout the continent. , As might be expected, loneliness set in. Weeks turned into months and months turned into years. With Brian's increased travel to take on more projects to finance and keep his wife happy, eventually he was home only a week or so each month. Soon affairs commenced with men she had met at various homes of the wealthy, and finally the marriage was over.

His wife had decided to move on through one of her encounters, an Englishman only working in Africa on a temporary basis. Now thirty, she was ready leave Africa and return with to London as a married woman to a wealthy gentleman. It was truly a dream come true. With her new wealthy husband life in Europe would be like a Lady of Letters, without concerns over safety and scarce amenities, which was the normal life of a white English Lady in South Africa.

After her departure, Brian became despondent, lonely, and took to drinking and servicing himself through prostitutes. A sad life at age 60. Geoffrey Wright knew this and knew Brian would go along with the requests regardless of legality.

Brian accepted this opportunity and shook hands with Geoffrey Wright, thus undertaking a challenge for which there was no turning back.

# CHAPTER 4
## *Alpha Team*

It was after midnight when the team assembled at the agreed-upon location, a dimly lit farmhouse. It was less than 5 miles from their target and used only during hunting season by a tourist safari lodge. Only Brian Smuts knew the identity of their financier for the evening's events. The room was cold. It was winter. Temperatures during the day climbed as high as 65 degrees, but after nightfall, the temperatures dropped rapidly. At times they could see the other's breath. The four of them were chosen for this operation because of specific skills.

Jako Steller, Mark Bethel, Jan Stein and Stephen Kennedy believed the purpose of their mission was to infiltrate Transgene for commercial espionage. Transgene had developed a HIV vaccine and another company wanted the formula to beat Transgene to the market, and if they couldn't, at least gain a hefty share of the market without the development costs. They all understood from Brian the goal was a no-traces break in. No one was to ever know that they came and went. Their understanding was they were being paid by another biotech company who wanted a clone of vaccine, and this was a simple in and out job against non-lethal private security.

The plan required four people for the necessary roles. First there was the need for a forward observer. This person would remain outside the Transgene perimeter fence with monitoring equipment. He would observe remotely and appraise the team of movements within the perimeter, whether they be Transgene employees or security personnel. That was Jako's job.

Jako's was a nickname for Jacob. He was raised in the Dutch Reformed Church (Van Niekirk) and Jacob was as biblical a name as they came. His family was very religious but Jako lost his faith after years as a soldier and then private mercenary. The latter was not about right or wrong, but how much you got paid. He was a former soldier in the South African Army and had fought in the Angolan wars. Divorced with no kids, and basically spending years as a Boer solider prior to the end of the Apartheid government, he was simply a loner. There was little left for him other than mercenary work from time to time as governments battled or uprisings in the countries such as the DRC, Mozambique or Equatorial Guinea required his skills.

He began his military career as a sniper in a forward observation position. He graduated to "forward placement of explosives," as his stealth skills become well known. His nickname was "The Ghost."

Sitting one day on his front porch somewhere on the Veld outside of Johannesburg, he contemplated the advertisement in the paper. It had been more than 15 months since his last work and aside from money, he needed to be occupied to prevent undue reflection on his lot in life. He was hopeful to snag a job without working with explosives. He looked down at his hand and thought how ironic it was that after 25 years in the military without injury, that he would now stare down at his left hand and see two fingers missing.

It happened 6 years prior during a mercenary operation into a military prison in Equatorial Guinea to rescue two British citizens accused of plotting to overthrow Mugabe in Zimbabwe. that itself was a total fiasco discovered during security preparations in route to Harare. He was working with a young Portuguese merc, a young lad, maybe twenty two, with sloppy explosives handling. The trigger was wired prior to placement box with Cemtex. Jako saw the wires were dangling out of the box and went to reset them. What he didn't know at the time was one of the wires had a split and copper was exposed. Jako went dark and when he awoke, he was in a hospital. In some sense he was lucky as the mission was a failure and he wasn't among those facing a firing squad. Fortunately, as with most things in Africa, for enough money, people were either released under some foreign nations plea for its citizens or enough money was paid to arrange a neat escape.

As a veteran, now taking courses for free at Wits (Witswatersrand University in Johannesburg), he bumped into an old mate from the Angolan war who was working for a technology contractor at one of South Africa's major diamond mines. The company specialized in heat sensing perimeter technology so the mines could prevent employees from sneaking out of the diamond fields.

What is it they say, "necessity is the mother of invention"? This company saw the need and modified a technology which came out the US's first Iraq war. It was refined and further developed over the past decade to distinguish between humans and animals by size, body movements, and more. The US DOD technology had been privatized and purchased by this SA firm.

In Johannesburg he took on this new skill with great zeal, obtaining a job with this firm via his war buddy. By delving into the training program to excel at this position, he had no idea how this new technology training would bring him to this day, rekindling his former skills as a forward observer while using a completely new non-lethal technology. He was truly ripe without knowing the requirements posted in the advertisement that read, "Seeking former military for private contract work. Must be single, no ties or family." He answered the ad via email at Ziffer@ziffer.de.

Second on the team was Mark. His job was to hack the security codes at the entrance to the facility. First, he was to use a portable 3D printer to generate plastic security cards so Jan and Stephen could move within the Transgene facility. It had been easy enough to hack into the HR encrypted file system to obtain the ID codes for personnel with access to secure areas and information. Next, it was his job to nullify camera surveillance by using a digital-loop-technique to create empty rooms and corridors when the team would be gaining entry into the containment room. That's where the primary clones for manufacturing the vaccines were kept.

Mark had begun his career as a systems analyst at IBM in 1992. He married, but unfortunately was shooting blanks. So he and his wife were considering adoption, bt that process is quite long. They stayed with it for several years, waiting to adopt a white baby from one of the former Soviet countries or possibly a Chinese baby. In either case the arrangements were long and protracted.

As he progressed at IBM moving from simple MIS to analytics, he was at the forefront of utilizing data for AI. Mark was able to see how digital technology could create data points to form pixel images indistinguishable from the real—holograms as it were. This was the skill needed in the 21st century as security was moving from video tapes to digital recordings.

Mark was a Princeton graduate. As the son of a military father, he was indoctrinated to serve America first before he served himself. It was his patriotic duty. His entire family had served militarily starting with his grandfather, who served in both WWI and WWII, to his father in Vietnam. After he enlisted in the Army and served in the first Iraq war and was honorably discharged, he began his first job at IBM, where WATSON and predictive analytics had begun. He was one of the brightest, but fortunes changed after a car accident led him to prescription pain killers and eventually, to hard drugs.

As with so many similar situations, it started innocently. In the early 2000s few understood how addictive a certain class of pain relievers were. Basically, they were a synthetic form of opiates. After 5 years of falling prey to the addiction, the expected results started to manifest. First it was his job, then debt from being out of work, then marital problems brought on by the protracted situation to adopt. He divorced and finally ended up a heroin addict living in a shelter. His path to responding to the advertisement, "Seeking single individuals with no family ties," was merely an accident.

He was at the VA that day, trying to see a doctor about getting onto the methadone program. While sitting in the waiting area he was reading the magazine, Soldier of Fortune, which sold lots of former military paraphernalia but also had a "Want ad's" section in the back. Mark read the ad. He knew of a friend who had taken an overseas job out in the Pacific Atolls, where there was no way he could come into heroin. He thought this advertisement might be his ticket to get straight, and out of his current circumstances. After all, like the advert noted, "Single, without ties or family," and he had nothing left, no family, no home and no money.

The last two individuals on the inside were Jan, acting as security fro the mission, and Stephen the geneticist. Jan was a former SA special forces. Despite the turmoil in the Middle East and its insatiable need for contractors, much of the private contract work outside that area was still taken up by former US soldiers and managed by US companies such as Blackwater. Given the Middle East was lit up like a Roman candle after 911 by George W. Bush, there was a lot of contract work to be had . The US had more discharged, out of work soldiers than any other country , so open opportunities were highly competitive! However, given the long Angolan war finally ending in 2002, there were also plenty of former SA soldiers teaming up with the US private contractors.

Blackwater was replete with highly skilled, unemployed soldiers not able to find work. Such an overabundance certainly brought down the salaries they had once commanded. Brian knew Jan was perfect, being South African, thus local talent for this job. The supply of former unemployed military forces was vast. Given the money involved, Jan would jump.

Jan had been regularly combing through internet sites seeking former military men as private contractors. In modern parlance, no one used the term *mercenary,* it was simply "Private Military Contractors." In his mid-fifties, he was still physically fit and a former Rugby player from his University days at Stellenbosch. He was built like a bull with a wide neck and broad shoulders. His style was as much a product of his physique as it was his former training—tough, rugged and able to break through anything. The perfect powerhouse to subdue and overtake any security personnel who might come upon them.

As a former military man, with his skills, he was the perfect backup and cover man for Stephen while he was working in the laboratory taking on his task to clone the vaccine. Jan was strong, but stealth was required for this mission. He had been trained by special forces in "Rendition Ops" to use medical sleep transducers. His kit contained liquid doses of powerful hypnotic tranquilizers. Once injected directly into the Carotid artery to create an artificial sleep, they allowed a complete interrogation under a state of drug induced hypnosis. The subject could have a scenario planted in their head to create "a blimp in time" from their perspective, which in fact may have been an hour without any cognition of the passing of time.

Stephen Kennedy was the last piece of the team, an American like Mark Bethel. He was the geneticist, whose job it was to copy the DNA and create a vaccine clone. Stephen was also another unfortunate and ripe for this mission as an out of work, 45-year-old geneticist. No wife, no home, no money and no ties! He had begun life working in a Biotech company after graduating from American University in Washington DC. His first job was involved with cleaving double stranded DNA while working on the Hepatitis B infectious vaccine.

It was a promising career in genetics both professionally and financially, as the field was skyrocketing in the early 2000s. However, trouble began during that same period with large pharmaceutical corporate acquisitions. Stephen's problem came in the form of, ultimately, a redundancy. Too many employees of similar skills who were no longer needed as divisions and companies consolidated. After the loss of his job through corporate consolidation, Stephen, as with Mark, had fallen on hard times trying to find work. He had already been through a divorce a few years before and the alimony and child support were truly burdensome. His wife had done quite a job on the kids, painting Stephen as a derelict father, therefore he also had no kids.

They were spoiled, and money ruled their alliances, and his wife kept that scenario going. He appealed to the court for alimony relief and was granted a 12-month period—or less if he found work, but the court had not granted relief on child support. From that point on Stephen had to do anything to generate child support or else he'd find himself back in court. Although it had been 5 years since the divorce, his wife had not grown more tolerant. She kept the pressure on him, threatening to take him back to court to force him to sell his condominium. At this point he had to sell the condo, but the proceeds were small as the mortgage was very high relative to the listed price. His net proceeds were about $20,000, just enough to pay the back ordered child support with a little left over to get into an apartment.

Stephen eventually had to take any work while still trying to find a professional position. He finally found short term work as a Limousine driver to bring in some form of money. It at least allowed him to start in the afternoon, and he tended to work until midnight or 1:00 AM at the latest. This kept his mornings free should he obtain interviews. The problem of being out of work when you made a great salary was no one wanted to hire you for less!

Stephen had been through many interviews. Some went the distance to three before he was flown to the corporate offices for the final HR look see. But each time it was to no avail. Stephen often networked with friends inside the company asking what happened? The answer he eventually got was always the same; they passed on you because you've made too much in the past and they fear that when an offer for what you are worth comes in, you'll leave!

So, one day while sitting at a call location, what he did after a dropoff instead of going back to base, he was reading the trade journal, "Genetic News," looking for work. In the journal he saw an advertisement which read, "Seeking experienced geneticist for overseas work. Need to be single, without ties or family." Respond to [Ziffer@ziffer.de](Ziffer@ziffer.de), Ziffer GMBH.

# CHAPTER 5
## *The Laboratory*

Jako succeeded in setting up the ID passes, Mark hacked the codes. Jan and Stephen were green-lit to enter the building using their magnetic ID cards to open digitally controlled door locks. Brian Smuts, through GRC who had been supplying research materials to Transgene, was able to get schematics on the layout of the building through the construction company who had built the containment labs. After all, in order to properly build containment labs, a schematic of the entire structure has to be provided to the construction company. And that company worked hand in hand with GRC who supplied the ventilation systems. It was simple enough to obtain access to the schematics from GRC's air filtration work seven years before when Transgene started their HIV vaccine project.

Jako had done his job. At this very moment, there weren't any technicians in the lab at this hour, but clerical work was still be done in some offices. The heat measuring systems profiled where everyone was and the instant they moved. In addition, Mark hacked into the network, allowing him to see who was working on their computers and when they logged on and off. They would know if anyone left their office space and headed toward the lab.

Two key scientist developers were working this evening despite it being past midnight. Jako, Mark and Jan were surprised but Stephen, being the geneticist, understood more than the others about the excitement of a project fulfilled, especially given the significance of their work. Most would be writing papers well into the future on techniques and processes that brought about their success. All no doubt expected newfound fortunes being highly sought by Biotech and pharmaceutical companies. Between Jako's heat identification system and Mark's hack into the central network, Jan would have the time to deal with any possible personnel interference. Once they got into the containment vault, Jan took his post and had his earpiece listening for any alerts from Mark or Jako.

Stephen's instructions were not only to copy the clone, but to make a rearrangement in the DNA of the vaccine. It wasn't overly difficult as he had all materials, like specific restriction enzymes, to be able to cleave the double stranded DNA chain. He could specifically target the code area where the vaccine was designed to create a new DNA to encapsulate HIV viral particles by making them susceptible to a new type of lymphocyte T-cells in humans. In this manner the human body would produce these new T-cells to specifically target the HIV molecule.

Stephen's problem now was one of time. To change the vaccine DNA he was using Polymerase Chain reaction known as PCR. It was considered by many to be the most important new development in the field of molecular biology since the discovery of restriction enzymes—the molecular "scissors" that selectively cut DNA. They had to be out of the facility before dawn. Stephen had to use a new technique which could accelerate the heating process to cut and remove the key component within the DNA strand and then put in place a different viral puck. His new technique was able, in only two hours of incubation, get the DNA separation and allow him to make the change to the vaccine.

The concept of a vaccine was to provide immunity through inoculation of a denatured virus that within the human body would form antibodies to fight off the disease and leave a resident immunity against it. What Stephen didn't realize was that the puck he was inserting was in fact the live virus. No doubt this was the actual plan to which no one on the mission was privy. All parties involved thought they were merely stealing a copy of the vaccine. Despite Stephen's personal situation, the idea of what he was actually doing would have been abhorrent. No rational being would contaminate a vaccine meant to save the world and turn it into a means of killing.

The Group of Six knew very well that Brian Smuts was given a live virus, but it was easily kept a secret as part of the molecular biotech materials kept in a sealed kit, not to be opened until they got to the lab. The idea that perhaps this might be dangerous for anyone on the team, let alone Stephen who would be handling the live infectious material, was of little consequence. For already determined by the Group of Six was that everyone on this team was disposable, and in fact they would each be disposed of once the mission was accomplished.

# CHAPTER 6
## *Home Free*

With the mission accomplished each person on the team received the money due them in their designated bank accounts. Each had new names to go along with their new passports. At this point, each man said their goodbyes and headed for the four winds. Brian Smuts made sure they each got out of South Africa via his contracted air transport dropping everyone in Kinshasa, DRC.

The DRC was chosen due to the constant turmoil in that country, which translated to, "it was easy to do anything with money." Jan headed back home to South Africa via a flight from Kinshasa to Gaborone, Botswana. He crossed the border into South Africa the same way he had left, via his land rover which he had stashed in Botswana. Jako was similar in that he had driven to Harare Zimbabwe from Johannesburg and left his car there as well. Zimbabwe was also like Kinshasa in the DRC. Bribery was easy due to the total collapse of financial institutions. It was so bad that local currency was better used for burning than for trade. In Zimbabwe, US dollars were the real legal tender, and in some instances, the South African Rand also had value.

Mark had other ideas. Sweden was a burgeoning market seeking talented persons for IT. Sweden was growing with enormous venture capital, and in a growth sector, there would be plenty of space for consultants. Although Mark did not speak Swedish, in Sweden all public schools taught English on a mandatory basis. A lot of venture capital was being thrown at AI, and Mark thought it was a good place to restart life with his own private AI consulting company. He now had 1.5 million dollars, and there was a shortage of people who were evolving within this new field.

For Stephen there were no thoughts of anything other than freedom. He was finally going on that long-awaited vacation for as long as the money held out. Stephen had no interest in any entrepreneurial enterprises. For him, it was time to restart life in all manners. He had decided to go and visit an old university mate, Max Brown, in Amsterdam. He and Max had met through intramural sports. That was Stephen's level of athleticism whereas Max was able to make the collegiate team, if only as a minor player. Max had become a journalist after school. He was working for the leading newspaper in Amsterdam, De Telegraaf. Stephen didn't speak Dutch but then again in Amsterdam, as it was for Mark in Sweden, everyone spoke English.

It was a perfect central place in Europe with ferries from the North Sea to the UK or a train to anywhere in Europe from "Centraal Station." This train station was the real heart of the city. Centraal Station was not only central by name but also the biggest public transport transfer spot, serving not only visitors to Amsterdam but the locals as well.

Stephen got on the train and headed for central downtown. His friend Max had an apartment above the Café Brasserie Stadsschouwberg on the Leidseplein. The Leidseplein was one of the major centers of Amsterdam nightlife and, on any night, throngs of young people could be seen coming and going from the many bars that sprinkled the area. Max had a great place in the middle of everything that was happening.

Stephen arrived around 4:30 and found, as expected, Max's place to be eclectic with all sorts of memorabilia. Max was a sports nut. From Basketball to Baseball, his collection was vast. He began his career in journalism as a sportswriter, and loved it. but wanted to cover more than stats for great athletes. He wanted to write about current events that affected the entire world. His father was a diplomat and as such Max had access to many politicians and other notable figures.

Max and Stephen had both attended Cornell University. Max's family covered the tuition, but Stephen had to get through on partial scholarships as well as holding down a part-time job. Max, given his family's money, was free to play sports. Although never a superstar, he was an avid sportsman in baseball and basketball, his favorites. Not overly tall but good enough to play a forward, although not first string. Despite lots of time on the bench getting splinters in his rear end, he enjoyed the scrimmages during the week even if he wasn't a starter. On occasion, after a good week of practice, he did get to start as a privilege to induce everyone, whether a starter or second-string player, to work their hardest during the week's practice. He was a better baseball player, but it was a slower game, and although he preferred it, he missed the fast pace of basketball.

Stephen enjoyed watching Max in games, and poked fun at his screw-ups. They met after a game at a fraternity party where Stephen pointed out that Max got three fouls in the first three minutes he was in the game. Max stood out in the Cornell game playing Syracuse, as no one could overlook this three foul performance. After Max was benched, Stephen noticed how he kept looking in the stands almost directly at him. However, he was looking at a girl two seats over.

His girlfriend was sitting right next to Stephen, and he could hear the laughter as the two girls joked about how annoyed Max was at being benched. Stephen introduced himself to the girl sitting next to him and asked about their jocularity at the guy who just got put on the bench. The other girl, sitting two seats down said she had just begun dating Max.

Stephen laughed again. "Max just wants to be the star, but just can't seem to make it no matter how hard he works."

"He's a good athlete," she demurred, "but he's not going to make the pros or anything. He needs to find a career in something else."

She was a sweet thing, and Stephen could tell she had a crush on Max big time.

"What are you doing after the game?" he asked the other girl.

"We're all going to a Fraternity party." She offered him a sneaky smile.

"Why don't you join us?"

Stephen laughed and thought how Max needed a wingman to clear the way with his new sweetie. He said yes to the invite with no hesitation. Let Max be surprised at the new addition to his night's plans. It was though Max's new girlfriend that they then became best friends.

Max and Stephen founded a great and deep friendship. As time went on, they became verbal sparring partners, and Max usually won. There was never a doubt in Stephen's mind, as their friendship grew, that Max was a gifted guy with words. So it was befitting that Max's career went toward sports media at first, and ultimately to current events journalism worldwide. It was part of the reason Max took this job in Europe with De Telegraaf.

After school when they graduated both he and Max stayed in contact via email and on occasion got together with friends for ski trips in Vermont, but their lives had changed as they often do for people moving further into their careers. Stephen got his first geneticist job in biotech, and their worlds grew further apart due to geographic distance. In addition, time for their friendship was greatly reduced as they both fervently pursued their respective careers.

Today, with huge hugs, Max was excited that Stephen was there on a prolonged visit. Max was single and enjoyed the fruits of becoming a somewhat noted American journalist working for De Telegraaf. When they finally sat down for a few beers, a girl came out from the bedroom hall. Max had been so excited at seeing Stephen he had forgotten to mention his sister was visiting from the states for a week.

Stephen's eyes were instantly riveted upon her. Sarah was about 5'7", slender, with long brown hair and a smile that could bring down the Berlin Wall—were it still in place. Sarah was seven years younger than Max, and when they were in school, she wasn't even a blip on Stephen's radar other than his friend had a younger sister.

She opened the frige, grabbed a beer and pulled up a chair to the kitchen table. After some brief smiles of embarrassment, as Stephen was trying not to stare, he turned to Max.

"I can't believe this is your kid sister, the one we made fun of all of the time. He lifted his glass. "How funny to see your sister after all of these years *here in Amsterdam.*"

As in Hans Christian Anderson's book, the ugly duckling had turned into a beautiful swan! There was no doubt, despite efforts to be low key, about the chemistry Sarah and Stephen felt with each other. The evening continued through reveling of great times in school, pranks, and reminiscing friends, parties, and professors. Finally, with enough alcohol and marijuana—Amsterdam is famous for it—they were ready to crash. Stephen said he was going to go over to the Kraznapolsky. It was one of the oldest and more famous in the Leidseplein area.

"Now wait a minute," Max said. "You can take my room. I'll sleep on the couch."

Stephen did respond rather immediately. "Well given how late it is, I'll stay. But *I'm* on the couch."

---

The next morning Max awoke first as he had a job and needed to be on the front lines to bring the world to De Telegraaf's readers! Sarah was still asleep in his second bedroom, and he tried to keep as quiet as possible with Stephen on the couch. However, Stephen heard Max and got up to share a cup of coffee. Max talked of the pieces he had been writing since 911 and now the more recent 711 attackt in London. His articles spoke of this new world and how life had changed in our public and open Western societies.

After a bit, Max saw his watch and realized the time. "Why don't you relax for the day. Maybe take my sister on a tour of the Ann Frank Museum. Then we'll all have dinner tonight."

Max was making light of Stephen's obvious excitement about his sister. But honestly, he couldn't think of a better fit for her than his old best friend. Max had no idea of Stephen's recent fall in life or the divorce or drugs. All he knew was that he was a noted corporate geneticist, not a guy who lost everything.

# CHAPTER 7
## *Thoughts of a New Life*

That morning, after Max left, when Sarah awoke, Stephen had already showered, cleaned up the couch, and was making a second cup of coffee. Sarah left the bedroom with a yawn.

"Well aren't we up very early."

"Indeed." Stephen went on to fill her in about his morning time with Max. "As we mentioned last night, how about we do the Anne Frank Museum and the Queen's Palace. What say you"?

"Sounds lovely by me, but let me get myself together, and we'll be off."

They left the apartment at 9:30 for the Anne Frank Museum. Upon arrival, they were awed by the photos, the collectibles, all that had been collected from the original attic. It was all emotionally stirring. The stories below each photo on the walls, as well as dioramas, made you feel as if you were living each day that Anne lived in that attic. Reading her actual notes mounted by the photos gave them chills as well as tears.

Neither of them had families who experienced the Holocaust. Sarah's Mom was Catholic, although her dad was Jewish. Stephen had the reverse, a Jewish Mom and a dad from Irish immigrants. Stephen was never sure if they were Jewish or not as his father was one of 11 and left his family at 16. There was never any closeness, and Stephen met his grandparents perhaps twice in his life.

# THE CURE

After they finished the museum tour, they went to lunch. It was an opportunity to get to know one another. Sarah began telling him about her work. She had graduated from nursing school and had been a nurse in NYC for four years. However she felt powerless as the system had not given her real opportunity to impact her patients. She was as altruistic as any could be dedicating her life's work to improving the human condition, if only a step at a time. After those four years Sarah felt she was not doing much more than taking vitals and measurements… She'd felt little more than a glorified monitor and record keeper.

She'd made up her mind to go back to school for a two-year degree to become a physician's assistant . After completing her degree she went to work for a non-profit NGO (Non-government Organization). A big part of her decision to go to work for a non-profit NGO was to run away. She had fallen in love with a young doctor while working at a hospital in NYC. He was an intern when they first met. They moved in together to share expenses, and as it goes, he then became a resident, and upon completion of his residency, within six months they split. So it wasn't a far step to consider leaving NY and taking a job overseas as a PA.

Her first assignment was in Uganda, traveling the rural areas attending improvised medical clinics. The clinics were nothing much more than old colonial buildings built from cinder block, with a century's worth of deterioration. They didn't even have any sort of reliable electricity. At a minimum these clinics served to address basic healthcare services like childbirth and testing for infectious diseases. The latter needed to be monitored regularly, since outbreaks could become pandemics and the WHO and other medical surveillance agencies desperately needed information for early intervention. Given the modern world of transportation, anyone could get on a plane and be on the other side of the world fully infected, for example, with the Ebola virus, which had an incubation time of as much as 48 to 72 hours without showing symptoms beyond the flu.

35

As the conversation went on, it was becoming glaringly obvious that Stephen had said nothing about his career and what he did. Stephen at this point felt it best to avoid the level of detail Sarah had offered. He probed, as best he could, to keep the conversation revolving around her, not knowing how to move further. She already knew through her brother that he was a geneticist working in biotech. However, Stephen said he had become a consultant in the past few years, adddding that it gave him a good deal of freedom to take time off when he needed mental space.

As the afternoon continued and they walked down the Dam Straat, Sarah's hand began bumping into Stephen's, and as one casual bump led to another suddenly their hands were clasped. Stephen thought it felt good and comfortable. Had he a telepathic helmet he would have known she felt the same. That type of chemistry needed no intuition or anything. The sentiments were quite clear. Sarah was as infatuated in Stephen as he was with her.

It seemed like a mere hour, but when they noticed the shade of the sun changing, they realized they had been walking for hours and talking incessantly.

Sarah then turned to Stephe. "Perhaps we should go back to the apartment and meet Max."

"Yes, it's best we have dinner together and celebrate the reunion." But Stephen needed to know one thing before they returned. "When are you leaving?"

"Five days."

Stephen was thrilled by her answer knowing he would have at least that long to be with her.

They had a splendid dinner that night at an Indonesian Rice Tafel, with tons of sweet and tangy little dishes. That type of food was quite common as the Dutch had many Malaysians living in Holland since the days when the Dutch were the primary explorers to the far east and places like Java, carrying spices back to Europe.

The next morning after Max went to work, Sarah and Stephen took Max's car and drove to the Hague. They walked along the sea and spoke more of their dreams for the future. Although only in her thirties, she agreed with him that time accelerated as one aged, at least in a way one could never understand in their twenties. It became apparent that the two of them were feeling each other out about the future. Despite the brief time they had been together, they were all too aware of the chemistry. They were giving signals through their words no matter how coy the conversation. Both were thinking, and wondering where the other saw it going.

At sunset, before the decision to head back to Amsterdam, they sat on a bench, looking out upon the sea. Stephen turned toward Sarah with her head leaning upon his shoulder, lifted her chin and kissed her. It was short, almost as if a surprise had fallen upon her, but their was great power behind it. She drew back, looked at him and lunged into a long, passionate kiss.

They drove the one hour ride with smiles, chatting back and forth, now with open fervor, as their feelings were known. Stephen was ecstatic, feeling warmth and a glow he had not felt with any other woman. It was almost as if his previous romances were all rehearsals, and this was where he got the part! Sarah too had been through her former relationship in NY, but this was different, and she could feel this was something special.

As the days sped by it was suddenly the last night that they would be together. The end of this unforeseen encounter was upon them. They were about to say goodbye, but neither was willing to let go. Sarah felt that to keep this night from being the last, she wanted intimacy. If not, then surely their chance meeting would lead to no shared future, given she was heading back to Africa.

After dinner at Max's flat, Sarah said, "Stephen, let's take some private time."

Max blushed as well as Stephen, but Sarah was taking control. If she were to hold onto this special chemistry between them, she would be dammed not to have them sleep together. As a woman who was once prepared to leave everything for Africa, her bravado was that of a person ready to act. Stephen saw this. It was part of her DNA—the ability to act! It was an attribute Stephen saw in himself, and he respected how they bolstered it in each other.

Sarah got up, looked at Max, then Stephen and reached for his hand. He took hers and let her guide him to the second bedroom. Stephen already knew Sarah was a woman to take charge. It wasn't as if Stephen lacked in this area, but on this he wanted her to take charge and lead the way. It was clear Sarah was not going to say goodbye and let this chemistry evaporate by distance and time. In her mind she saw no impediments to a future relationship as Stephen wasn't grounded to any specific job, and once she finished in Uganda, only 6 months to the end of her tour, they could be together.

As Sarah led them into the room, Stephen closed the door. She turned to face Stephen and he pulled her close, engaging her in a long, slow kiss. They nudged as if slow dancing closer to the bed and like two Swans they glided into it together. As their warm and soulful kisses continued, so did the removal of their clothes.

Once they were each bare, Stephen looked at her graceful contour and slowly caressed her beautiful breasts, kissing them gently. Their hands began to roam and explore each other's loins. He touched her gently between her legs as she did with him. The additional contact ignited their passions further, and ignited her desire for Stephen to be inside her. He pressed her flat to the bed, got on top and entered her. The warmth and wetness were as it was with their first kiss, beyond anything he ever knew. Sarah pushed his shoulders up a bit and stared at his face as they climaxed together. In exhaustion they laid side by side as all lovers do, staring up at the ceiling in euphoria. Sarah, while staring at the ceiling thought to herself, this was not simply an act of sex but true lovemaking like she had never known before.

After catching her breath, Sarah said, "Are we going forward from here, Stephen? Certainly we aren't going to let this go." She nuzzled her head into his shoulder and moved tightly to his body.

Stephen took a few seconds, which can sometimes seem like an eternity. "We'd be idiots not to follow what we've found between us. This encounter, our meeting is almost beyond propinquity. While your life had been buried in Africa and mine on a bit of a decline the last few years, with the money I've just accrued from my last consulting project, we could go and set up a life anywhere."

"What kind of consulting project would have had a payoff so large that we could retire and start life anew elsewhere?" Sarah asked.

Stephen avoided a direct answer. "I'll tell you about it in the future, but for now, suffice it to say, it was work on a new vaccine that had great commercial value worldwide."

He felt a bit guilty in not telling her the truth, but this was not the time for details that has a chance of scarring her off, after all it was merely commercial espionage. No one was hurt. The world is full of greed, and if he did not participate, surely, they would have found someone else.

He shut down this line of thinking before continuing. "Tomorrow we'll give some thought on how to meet at some destination when you complete your contract." Stephen thought that might be anywhere outside of Europe. Maybe New Zealand.

As they continued to lie together, Stephen thought how amazing the universe was. How strange that as one door closed, another opened. Here he'd found the love of a lifetime, and with one million dollars in the bank. He felt her body next to his. A life with Sarah was a wonderful dream.

she was not some strange person from a bar, or an online encounter, but his oldest friend's sister.

He turned to Sarah, unaware that while he had been talking, she fell asleep. He dozed off into sweet dreams of the future they would now share.

# CHAPTER 8
# *World Health Organization Approval*

At 9:00 AM Geneva time, every news network broke for a major breakthrough announcement on a HIV Vaccine. All hands were on deck, CNN, NBC, Der Speigel, Der Telegraffe, La Monde, et al gathered in the auditorium at the WHO headquarters. No one was sure exactly what the announcement would be. Would it be a breakthrough on a cure? Perhaps one hundred media persons and dignitaries were there for this announcement. Many major Pharmaceutical corporation heads were in attendance, from Merck to Johnson & Johnson, from Sandoz to Eli Lilly.

The room was a abuzz with rumors as the media waited for the participants to assume the dias. To the left was a lectern where the press secretary for the WHO was shuffling papers. At 9:30, the press secretary for Dr. Salvadore Genovese, the head of the infectious disease department at WHO, took to the microphone at the center of the dias and announced they were about to begin and asked the crowd to bring the din down in the hall so they may proceed. As Dr. Genovese and four others took to the dias, he opened his papers from the center of five chairs and looked about the room.

Genovese was a team player, and it was he who instructed that a dias be set up this way as he did not want to be the main focus as the announcement. He was a career infectious disease doctor and had person-

41

ally been the champion in the search for an HIV vaccine. As he prepared to speak he thought the day as grand as he could have imagined, creating a cure that would endure mitigating the crisis of this pandemic spreading throughout Africa.

He scanned the crowd. "Ladies and Gentlemen I am here today to let the world know we now have completed our test trails for an HIV vaccine." The room immediately went abuzz. "Transgene, a South African Biotech company. developed this vaccine in conjunction with the assistance of the WHO facilitating the testing sites. As of now we are prepared to launch it."

The crowd went into a flurry of gesticulation, clapping and reaching for the sky. The press corps began screaming questions with such a furor that it was impossible for Dr. Genovese to continue to speak.

The incredible clamor drew the press secretary to the podium, and he spoke into the microphone. "Please, everyone, calm down." He stepped away, allowing Dr.

Genovese back to the podium.

"Ladies and Gentlemen, as cited before this is a historic moment."

A reporter shouted, "When will this vaccine be put into use?"

The noise from the rest of the media almost drowned out the question. The doctor held his hands up and again asked for quiet.

"No doubt your question, Ms. Maccabe of the BBC, is shared by everyone else in the room. The answer is *immediately*. We will begin next month. At this point logistics is the critical factor to move forward. The identification of key clinics which can accommodate large groups, distribution of the vaccine, staff required, as well as dealing with governments to avoid impeding the movement of the vaccine from country to country as well as protection and security for the shipments. The WHO will be working directly with Transgene to ensure manufacturing is up to speed so that we may inoculate up to 250,000 people per month. Thanks to donations from numerous foundations, given Transgene's existing manufacturing facility, we expect that within 12 months they will double the production capacity and be able to reach 3 million persons the following year. With the assistance and pledges from private sector donors we believe that Transgene will be able to build a new factory with a higher speed production capacity to perhaps be able to more than double that amount within one year. We're all very optimistic and encouraged by what we saw when we visited Transgene during our Beta testing."

Dr. Genovese went on to introduce the founder and CEO of Transgene,. Dr. Seymore Berger, and the company's chief scientist, Neil Steinbrenner.

Dr, Berger stepped to the podium amid the roar of shouted questions and loud applause. Eventually holding his hands up, everyone quieted down to permit him to speak. Dr. Berger knew just how to work an audience. First, he allowed 10 seconds of silence as he scanned the room to insure everyone felt they had eye contact.

"I'd like to thank my team and of course all of the people at the WHO have worked so diligently with Transgene. This has truly been a team effort with other pharmaceutical companies, the WHO and International Governments. At this time, I'd like to introduce Dr. Neil Steinbrenner. It was Dr. Steinbrenner who identified the sequence in the DNA of the HIV virus that led us to the final piece which allowed the success of our vaccine. We're calling the Vaccine "Brenovo" as a tribute to Dr. Steinbrenner."

Steinbrenner stepped up with a gesture by Genovese. "In simplistic terms," he started, "the mechanism we discovered in the CD4 cells allows us to simply switch the virus off and allows our own immune system to do direct battle with the virus when HIV is contracted."

After Steinbrenner finished, Dr. Genovese announced a Q & A period.

As this was a sensational event, all of the cable networks were carrying the announcement live. At the men's club in St. James, Nigel Jones and Roger Atwood were listening quite intently.

As the Q & A began, Nigel turned to Roger with a very sinister smile. "The games have begun."

"I have no doubts," Roger replied, "that as we imagined, the corrupt leaders of our former colonies will be the first to be inoculated."

"Indeed. I suppose we need to convene our group and move to the next stage. That is eradicating those involved to ensure there are no surprises and no trails to be followed when things begin to fall apart in 90 days.."

"I would imagine it will take at least 30 days of investigation if not more to see there is an issue with the vaccine," Roger mused.

Nigel lifted his martini towards Nigel in a gesture of a toast. "I'll get the Group of Six convened at the earliest possibility."

# CHAPTER 9
## *Death is Becoming Common*

Saturday afternoon was sad, but held great optimism for the future of Sarah and Stephen. At Schiphol airport, Sarah was about to get on a plane.

"Email and who knows," Stephen said, "you may just find me showing up in Kampala next week. I have a few details to take care of on finances but other than that, my life is free as a bird." Stephen watched as she boarded, and did not leave the airport until he saw the jet taxi to the runway.

As Stephen drove home, his heart was aglow.

*How lucky can a guy get?*

When he arrived back at Max's apartment it was about 5:00 and Max was already there. He was going to go to the airport with them but realized the two love birds needed their goodbye alone.

When Stephen entered, Max said, "It's time for me, your old friend. What say we go out to celebrate you and Sarah and perhaps a lifetime together."

They grabbed their coats and went to one of Max's favorite pubs. While sitting at the bar and regaling about old times, Stephen kept interjecting Sarah. Just as they were on their second beer Stephen noticed some news on the TV. A car accident. It was nothing to really take notice of but when they showed a photo of the victim, Stephen choked.

"Are you okay mate?" Max asked.

"Yeah, but the guy who they just showed on the news is someone I was just working with in South Africa. He was a supply chain manager, and he was the one who recruited me. Wow, geez. What bad luck." Brian had also just gotten his payday on the work they did.

As they continued to drink, Stephen came to a conclusion fitting the night's activities. "Let me toast to the guy." Stephen, feeling quite flush. announced loudly to the bar that a friend of his was just killed in an accident, and that he wanted to buy a round of drinks for everyone to toast him. And so he did. Stephen raised his glass and yelled, "To Brian, ach ne kock man. He was a good mate"!

Max did not think it odd that a local news station would carry a car accident in Johannesburg. The close ties between the Netherlands and South Africa went way back to colonial times, as it was in Great Britain with America. Cape Town was Holland's

first settlement to allow its ships in the 16th century to restock provisions before the next leg to Malaysia. So it was not unusual for local Dutch networks to carry news from South Africa as trade, families and social ties between those two countries were still very strong despite the fall of the Apartheid government.

Of the white population in South Africa, about 50% were of Dutch ancestry and became known as the Boers, while the other 50% were of English ancestry. After the toast, Max and Stephen returned home smiling despite Stephen's sad and unsettling surprise news. The next day, Sunday, was leisure and Max showed Stephen the insider places of Amsterdam, the places that only the locals frequent. It was a good day and they ended up at the home of one of Max's friends for Braai, that is

Dutch barbecue. Monday Max went to work, and Stephen got to planning his new life with Sarah.

In the morning Stephen wrote his first of many emails to Sarah. The reply was almost immediate. As the weeks went by Stephen realized she was quite involved in her work and were he to fly to Uganda and show up, it would be an imposition. Sarah's work was important to her. She wanted to focus on it exclusively that she might finish strong and start her new life together with him without any regrets. As it would be another four months until Sarah's obligation to the NGO was completed, Stephen set out to occupy himself for the months ahead.

He was busy looking at search engines for Biotech firms involved in vaccines thinking perhaps he could get some part time work in a laboratory. Fortunately, while there was no part time work, he did see a advert for a copy writer. A pharmaceutical publication wanted someone to take raw data and convert it into a lay format for non-academics.

"Well, certainly I can edit raw data and convert it into legible information."

He applied by e-mail, got an instant reply, and a meeting was set for the following week. At the meeting Stephen's CV was more than enough for anyone to see he had the research background. They offered him the job saying they expected the work load to be completed within three to four months. When they asked if the pay was sufficient, Stephen inwardly smiled. He'd have done it for nothing to simply keep myself busy for the next few months.

After two weeks, life fell into a routine. Stephen and Sarah connected frequently using facetime and Skype, choosing whichever worked best given the available bandwidth limitations in Uganda. Stephen rented a car on a month to month basis. The only drawback to his work was its location in Zootemeer. a small hamlet on the way to the Hague. It was a lovely ride though the country, but it took fifty minutes to an hour depending on the traffic getting out of the city.

Getting into his car on the Monday of the second week he didn't notice anything odd about the way the car was handling. Once outside of the city, he accelerated to about 110 KPM and in an instant the wheels went wide. The steering was gone, and the car skidded off the road into a grassy area. After what seemed an eternity, although only ten seconds, the car ground to a halt. He closed his eyes trying to catch his breath and then he exited to inspect the front end. Both wheels were pointing away from the car.

With a certain amount of calm, he called the Dutch equivalent of AAA, a service provided by the car rental company. When the service truck showed up, the driver took the hook to the front of Stephens car and hauled it onto the platform. As the service engineer strapped it down, he had full view of the front axle. His eyes grew wide.

"Someone has been at your axle. It was not a break. It looks to me as if someone cut seventy five percent through the bar, allowing the stress of the drive to finish it off." Stephen was shocked and wondered why anyone would tamper with is car. The service technician continued. "Either the rental agency was at fault or someone tampered with the axle."

Perplexed but undaunted, Stephen went off to the office in Zootemeer by taxi and took a bus and train home that evening. At the apartment, he recanted the entire story to Max.

His response was, "That's insane!"

The next day the rental agency supplied another car but there were questions as their repair garage had to fill out a request for replacement parts and explain for insurance purposes what had happened. The service manager at the rental agency felt something was not right but couldn't imagine who would do such a thing if in fact it was tampering with the car.

As it all seemed so suspicious, he called the insurance agent for the rental agency and in turn the insurance agent sent an adjuster to examine the vehicle before any work was done.

He inspected the axle. "Who was the renter of the car?"

An American working in Holland for a few months," the service manager answered. "He had a month to month rental."

The next day the adjuster called Stephen and asked if he could come by to speak to him about the accident. When they met at Max's apartment, Stephen went into a full detail about what he had seen, which was exactly what the tow driver had seen.

"Stephen, would anyone be interested in harming you?"

Stephen shrugged. "No!"

He couldn't imagine anything like that as he didn't really know anybody in Holland other than Max. The adjuster took notes and considered other explanations, perhaps related to the previous renter of this specific vehicle.

That night at dinner Stephen told Max all about the adjuster, what was found, and the uncanny theory about how it must be related to the previous renter. Max was wowed, imagining something intriguing beyond an accident, but they simply laughed it off and thought how lucky Stephen was not getting killed.

"Geez imagine if something happened to you," Max offered, "considering your friend was just killed in a car accident." Upon those words out of Max's mouth, did the two of them suddenly looked at each other in silent acknowledgment. Max reached his hand across the table. "Stephen, is there something going on in your life I don't know about? Isn't it too much of a coincidence? Y Your friend was just killed in a car accident and now this? Whether it was meant for you orthe previous renter, what are the odds?"

There's no way it's connected, Stephen answered. "It's got to be a fluke."

That night before Stephen went to sleep, he spoke with Sarah and of course she was concerned, and happy Stephen was alright.

"No harm, no foul," she said.

It was those words that resounded in Stephen's mind. *No harm no foul...* It continued to weigh on him into the night.

"What are the statistical odds of untimely deaths of two team members within two weeks who were involved in commercial espionage?"

For Stephen that night was the beginning of many restless ones to come.

# CHAPTER 10
# *The Government Terrorist Model?*

It was 2001, only months after 911. All of America was living in disbelief and fear. America had never been attacked on its own shores, but now the world had become smaller and we were even calling French Fries American Fries. So much changed. The world, especially the US, became overshadowed by the dark cloud of fear. Like a mist drifting down the aisles of a movie theater, unseen but nevertheless insidious. As the US became a paranoid nation, given this was a first time strike on their insulated shores,

Concurrent to this visceral attack on the mainland, white envelopes with an unknown white powdery substance began showing up at Congressional offices, the homes of elite corporate executives, and at postal centers. It was immediately defined as Anthrax, a virus that evolved through the Bovine species. Once verified, there was only one institution in the US that maintained a biohazard level four containment unit authorized to hold such a viral substance. It was located at Fort Detrick in Maryland.

And so began the FBI's manhunt for who was perpetrating these new and ongoing terror attacks in America. After much examination of the various envelops, and tracking posting routes, the FBI determined the source of the Anthrax was the lab at Fort Detrick.

It was in the 1970s that the United States government began to experiment with the virus as an infectious agent for bio-viral warfare once it was found to be profoundly deadly to humans. The next step the FBI took was to investigate who had access inside the lab to the virus. Once that was determined, background checks were done on all these individuals prior to commencing interrogations.

It was an all out hunt within this level 4 biohazard lab. In a short period of time, it was found that Bruce Edward Ivins, a microbiologist, had been working on this deadly Anthrax strain for a few years. But there was no clear trail. The strain had been sent out for testing by the most secretive agencies inside the US government. No errant trails or mishandlings were found. Who would ever consider the idea of bio-viral warfare, short of terrorists? The FBI investigated for months, desperately trying to find a trail. But in the end, they proceeded no further than Bruce Ivins. When there is no one to blame, and nowhere to go, find a scapegoat.

Clandestine agencies deep in the bowels of governments are not a new concept, but digitized documents were a new way to keep them hidden. No one inside the FBI had to think farther back than the McCarthy era or Hoover to see how, given the 911 attack and the current paranoia, that an arrest was imperative and critical to put the population at ease. So it was that Bruce Edward Ivins was falsely accused of sending Anthrax through the mail as no trails led to anyone else due to the perfectly hidden tactics of this internal US government clandestine group that was never to be found. They were responsible for sending the Anthrax letters. Their purposes no doubt was to intimidate those who would have blocked the development of this Bio warfare strategy. As with many secrets of history, the truth was at least decades, if ever, to be discovered.

It wasn't until 2003 that Bruce Ivins was finally acquitted, but during those two years the US Federal government falsely accused him of beginning a domestic terrorist program. The US government made Mr. Ivin's life unbearable, including a portion of time spent imprisoned. He was cleared by evidence proving he had properly managed and handled the virus protocol, despite those plotting against him in order to have shown to America that they had caught the terrorist.

After that, his life was never the same. He committed suicide in 2008. He was nothing but a casualty of a government that never solved the crime but ruined a man's life, and the political aspirations of those who had been tasked by the FBI under the Bush administration to find someone. Once the envelopes ceased arriving at critical government desks, the FBI could have quietly left things in a mode of ongoing investigations, the kind no one ever brings up again. The actual terrorist was never found.

# CHAPTER 11
## *Group of Six Consolidation*

As the weeks went by the Group of Six worked easily to ensure that each of their enlistees were eliminated; Brian Smutts, Jako Steller, Mark Bethel, Jan Stein and Stephen Kennedy. Accidents were an easy enough to generate when the right authorities were paid enough. Even autopsy or police reports could be *encouraged* to cite no foul play. The Group of Six were seeing their plan to reclaim Africa coming to fruition.

However, Stephen Kennedy seemed to have eluded their attempt to terminate his existence and disappeared. With all of their resources they had not yet been able to locate him after the first mishap where he survived the attempt to crash his car. Now the Group was beginning to be quite concerned regarding this loose end. Although the Group of Six, under Nigel Jones direction, had eliminated every other team member, Kennedy remained elusive. It seemed he went underground and was nowhere to be found. Finding Kennedy was key to the success of the Group. Everyone must be eliminated to ensure no trail led back to them and the plan.

As usual the Group turned to Nigel seeking a solution to Kennedy given none of the Group's resources had been successful since the first failed attempt. Nigel pondered the imponderable. How to find someone who was desperately trying not to be found. After all the group selected each of these men because they had no ties to family or anyone.

Nigel sat back in his study, staring out of his window looking onto the lustrous grounds of his estate, and gave thought to this problem. It seemed in order to resolve this issue they would require an intense amount of manpower. Resources beyond those at the Group's disposal of well paid private agents. Many were former SAS, Interpol, Legionnaires or even the formidable East German Spetznaz. But in each case, while they had many connections inside their former organizations, none retained any deep access to inside records or ongoing investigations. Yes, they had their inside moles, but it was not the same as being inside on a formal team. Other than phone calls to friends, their registered official life was over.

"What we need is a crisis," he mused, "to get government agencies moving and give our people access to leaks."

Leaks always became more prevalent when there was a crisis. Official organizations were constantly plagued by the media's internal sources. It was a two-way street. When any inside government official needed help, they knew where to go to get anonymous information and in return the media obtained unreleased information or first rights to a big story in return. They worked together on a limited basis, forming a symbiotic relationship between government and media. Each needed the other.

In his thinking of significant world crises, 911 certainly was the biggest terrorist undertaking. He then remembered the pandemonium in America during the Anthrax scare which began shortly after the 911 attack in New York. Perhaps it was Nigel's experience from his early days at the Bar as a barrister moving him in this direction of devious and strategic thinking. In the past, leaks had assisted him as a prosecutor convicting hardened criminals, and sometimes acquitting them.

Kennedy had been quite elusive. Nigel thought hard to come up with a solution. *How do you find what doesn't want to be found?* The answer came to him in manner akin to his favorite Detective, Sherlock Holmes.

Holmes would always use deduction to find something hidden. To find the unknown, one must first eliminate the knowns.

Thinking in this manner he came to see that no matter how many private agencies he might employ to locate Kennedy, no one had the resources of governments. Their deep data bases, their ability to track all persons moving from one border to another, by car, train or by air. Borders must be crossed. Credit cards get used, banks get visited, clothes get cleaned and people eat in restaurants. However, how to entice governments to assist them? He would have to consider their motivating interests, the Group of Six's motivations for taking back Africa's assets, and how they would align. Western governments could be made to put their resources to finding Stephen Kennedy.

Geo-political motivations to hunt someone, and indirectly aid the Group, might be "risk to human lives." However, in reality, the Western nations would be more concerned with the Chinese and their slow take over of Africa by lending billions to poor countries in exchange for long term mineral rights. Here he saw the alliance.

Were there scruples in Western nations? Not really, but given there would be millions of lives lost to a pandemic and how the liberals would be overly concerned with saving lives, there would be a huge outcry to find the culprit or culprits of some white nationalist terrorist prepared to kill millions. In truth the West would only be interested in their geo-political position. After all, Europe has been invaded by refugees fleeing Africa and the total break-down of governments. Syria, Libya, Egypt, Palestine, Somalia, Iraq, Iran, Yemen with Huthi rebels fighting and Saudi Arabia trying to ensure their side-maintained control—basically the entire middle east was a tinder box.

Farther south, from Sierra Leone to Uganda, to Kenya, to Zimbabwe and even South Africa—the latter once being the pearl of Africa. Now it was crumbling from lack of spending on infrastructure by its corrupt ANC government which continued to ignore the disintegration of their nation while being busy stealing the sovereign wealth of the nation. These days of brown outs were so frequent from lack of sufficient electricity, that most factories and businesses have had to operate 3-day work weeks.

Truly Nigel thought, were the liberals to think it through, they probably would have said, *let the Europeans take back the continent*. Nigel thought the plan brilliant. The Group of Six would hide in plain sight with the West assisting our plan! Yes, the Vaccine was already in play confirmed by the WHO. The African leaders were the first ones in line getting it, ostensibly to prove to their countrymen the safety thereof. The reality was as Nigel expected of these cheap despots allowing despair amongst their "so called" brethren while they stole from their country and salted away billions in Swiss banks, like Mugabe and other notable leaders. In fact, the Western governments internally knew the real reasons for their intervention was Western self-preservation with little concern regarding the population as a whole once they were inoculated.

Nigel felt the best way to get the Western governments to unknowingly assist the Group's plan was to leak out that Stephen Kennedy was the head of a radical European national terrorist organization who had tried to break into the facility manufacturing the HIV vaccine but failed. That Kennedy was an out of work bio geneticist lent itself even further credibility to the narrative that he had compromised the production of vials into which the vaccine had been inserted. The glass vials had been clandestinely produced out of an old, shutdown Romanian state-owned pharmaceutical facility. That his group had produced hundreds of thousands of vials prepared even before the WHO announcement and had been transported by ship into Africa and then distributed to Transgene by truck.

The story line would be that through the company providing the sterilization process for the vials, he had paid off a worker whose job it was to introduce a glycerol coating after sterilization. This was to prevent the vaccine from crystalizing under the heat it might be exposed to during transport within various countries, as refrigerated trucks were in short supply. However it was *not* this glycerol coating that went into the vials after sterilization but rather a substance which would have the reverse impact to the vaccine's DNA, creating a new, deadly antigen which would strengthen the HIV virus.

So, without knowing where the contaminated vials were in the ongoing distribution process, how would the authorities investigate without introducing panic for those who have already been inoculated? Nigel thought to leak his narrative through the group's well-paid media contacts to the Western Government. It seemed clear to Nigel. Generate documents, emails, texts, CGI altered CCTV footage, messages and build and imaginary cabal!

First, he would leak it out to the international press using an anonymous contact. Just a small drip of information and then it would become a press feeding frenzy. It would be easy for the Group to plant communications to validate Stephen Kennedy as a radical on the loose, and that he must be found with all due dispatch.

Nigel smiled and laughed to himself. The irony of it all. The ingeniousness of getting the world out front in what they had done and blaming it on Kennedy, while all of the time the real vaccines produced by Transgene were in fact the ones genetically altered to put all inoculated into their death throws within sixty days after inoculation. Simply brilliant!

Governments chasing Kennedy, trying to prevent him from supplanting the real deadly vaccine with an imaginary deadly vaccine that didn't even exist. Nigel relished the beauty of Western nations pretending they are saving the world when in fact acting in their own self-interest to move on Africa. The world would see that it was the West that saved nations, not China. The Western Nations could be made to look like the saviors of Africa.

Nigel, having completely laid out this plan in his mind, rang Roger Atwell. He explained his ingenious thinking to bring governments of the world to work for the Group of Six in finding Stephen Kennedy. He told Roger to contact Fritz, as he was the chairman, to arrange an emergency meeting of the Group. After the call Nigel thought how his hero Sherlock Holmes, the great detective, had been his inspiration for this strategy by looking the association of goals between the Group and the Western nations. Perhaps it was a strategy that barristers needed to employ against overwhelming odds to get their guilty clients off that had led to his proposal to the Group of Six. As always, he seemed to be the great thinker.

The following week the group of Six met in Austria at Fredrick Dressler's retreat. All were there; Roger Atwell, Franz Herens, Fritz Kronner and Roger Collier. Once seated and pleasantries finished, Fredrick stood and turned the floor over. Nigel Jones began by retelling the story of Bruce Edward Ivins and the Anthrax scare and the subsequent hunt by governments all over the world to assist in locating this terrorist. He went on to cite how the world had become ever more paranoid after 911, perhaps rightfully so, and that all governments were now are cooperating on intelligence matters far beyond the levels of 2001. He explained that their solution to find Stephen Kennedy was the governments of the world conscripted as our unknowing hunters.

"With our strong connections to the media, leaking our story will be easy," Nigel said. "We can move ahead of government agencies with our own moles at Interpol and take him out ourselves when he is located. With enough money, we'll be able to see to it that our Interpol contacts will be very aggressive to insure he will never be captured alive."

"It all sounds too simple," Fredrick said.

"We already have all of the right people in Interpol on our payroll. Once we get them working with government agencies, is there anyone in this room who doesn't see how the West will keep it quiet to avoid panic while the Transgene inoculations are being implemented throughout Africa? If anyone suspected that there was a radical white European group trying to switch the real vaccine for a contaminated one there would be pandemonium. Gentlemen, the *cure* is almost upon us!"

# CHAPTER 12
# *Sleepless Nights*

After several sleepless nights, Stephen began doing internet searches on recent deaths in countries where he knew the former team members had scattered. He was sure none of his former teammates would be using social media. After learning Brian Smutts was in the car accident, the first to be found in his search was Mark Bethel. Mark was the easiest to find online as Stephen knew he was headed for Sweden as a topflight hacker. That's where he planned to take his money and set up a consulting business. It seems Mark's car lost control in Goethenberg and went into a frozen lake where he was found and identified within the week of Stephen's unfortunate car incident.

*Only two left...*

Jako Stellar and Jan Stein were not to be found, but given Mark's and Brian's fate, and the attempt on himself, he had little doubt that Jako and Jan were already dead. But then again, they were former military and who knows to where they disappeared. But as former mercenaries, no doubt their disappearance would go unnoticed.

At this point, after reading about Mark, Stephen was quite convinced they would not stop coming after him. Surely, he now understood the plot. His research showed the company he was supposedly involved with had suddenly disappeared. Stephen searched high and low throughout the internet and nothing ever appeared regarding Ziffer GMBH. Then he typed in Ziffer@ziffer.de and the results were *error 404*. He knew then it was a set up and doubted he'd live to spend his million dollars.

While he hadn't seen anyone following him, he had no doubt they were on his rear and only looking for the right moment to lurch upon him. He tried contacting the Chamber of Commerce in Germany. They too said, "never heard of them." He tried to understand the purpose of the mission. It now seemed perhaps industrial espionage might not have been the only reason, as why would you kill those who helped you make a fortune.

He started to get the bad feeling that he hadn't just changed the formula to be ineffective to beat a competitor to market. He tried to go back over what he had actually done in copying the material. The gene map he was given to replace the DNA sequence at Transgene came from GRC. He then went online to search for GRC Biomedical supplies. They too didn't exist!

*God only knows what I replaced in the new DNA sequence.*

With a frightened thought, given the deaths around him and the less than savory Europeans that were trying to push back the refugee problem in Europe, could there be a more sinister plot regarding the changed DNA sequence? Vanguard countries such as the Czech Republic, Hungary, Poland and Slovakia were not interested in becoming the African refugee landing zones that Greece and Italy had become.

He considered the HIV problem in Africa and began to believe a dark conspiracy was possible. He recalled the World Health Organization (WHO) announcement of the vaccine. When he had read it, he hadn't paid any attention to the name of the company who developed the vaccine. Now he realized *he* had most likely rearranged the vaccine so it would become toxic and he was a liability to the plotters of this scheme.

Was the name Transgene? Did he omit from his memory that company name where he replaced the DNA sequence on his supposed industrial espionage venture? He immediately then went back online to the WHO website to find the name of the company who was supplying the vaccine. Sure, enough it was Transgene.

*Did I do more than simply steal a functioning DNA sequence for the HIV vaccine?*

The next thought was he had to get to the authorities. If he was right, he rearranged the sequence not to fail—but inserted a sequence to kill!

He decided, with nowhere to go, to tell Max everything, literally everything about his life, fall from the world, lost marriage and answering the ad for a bio geneticist. Stephen got up from his desk and went into the living room when Max was watching a football match.

"Max, I've got to talk to you now." Stephen proceeded to tell Max about what had really been going on in his life. "It seems I've been involved in something very far from legitimate." He explained the recruitment, Ziffer GMBH, GRC medical distributors and how nothing existed online anymore. "Max, I got paid one million dollars! It was no accident with my rental car as the insurance adjuster suspected." He wound down and mused to himself. "Jesus, where do I go on this now?"

Max incredulously stared at Stephen after this huge dump on his life for the past 5 years. Add to that this illegitimate break-in where Stephen was the lynch pin on changing the DNA sequence on the HIV vaccine. Considering the deaths of those who went on the mission with Stephen, the conclusion was obvious.

"Stephen you're in some very deep shit here mate!" "Perhaps we should reach out to the authorities?

"No," Stephen said. "The likelihood is these people are very connected. Going to the authorities would only lead them to me. The people behind this plot are working with Western governmental authorities under some guise and would surely get to me first. Then I'm a dead man! Somehow, I've got to go deeper to see if in fact what I did was to implant a poison pill so to speak. Once confirmed, we'll have to yell it from the highest public rooftop for my safety."

Stephen realized staying underground was all that was left to him until he could figure out what to do.

Max said, he would "I'll check all the international press wires tomorrow," Max said. "Don't go to work and stay in the house until I get back."

# CHAPTER 13
# *A Woman to the Rescue*

Max's return brought no new information regarding anything unusual related to Transgene or the HIV Africa vaccine front. Stephen had been in the house all day waiting. They ate quietly.

"Max, I've got to get out of here as they obviously know where I am based on the car incident, but perhaps not sure where to go from there." He looked Max in the eye. "Brother, we're old friends and the last thing I want to do is endanger Sarah, but to me it seems heading to Uganda might be the smartest thing as she is there. But I'd like your permission before I go and get her involved. I've no doubt she will be if they are chasing me!"

"First things first," Max said. "We've got to get you some documents so you can get on a plane and we definitively don't want it in your name."

"How?"

Max grinned, "You can't be in the newspaper business without having contacts, criminal ones that is. I'll fill Sarah in as who knows if your email is safe. What if this secret cabal had somehow sent you a text with a link from one of the job ads you responded to and it had an encryption deep inside. When you opened it, maybe that's how they knew where you rented a car because they caught your reply for the interview."

Max seemed in thought for a moment, as if steeling himself for a dramatic course change. ""First let's get you documents, a new ID, passport, driver's license, and then out of Amsterdam. By the time you show up in Uganda, Sarah will have the complete story from a secure encrypted email at my Newspaper. We maintain encryption services due to the nature of our sources. We must keep their identity secret if we want them to continue working with us. If we didn't do that, imagine how many sources we could convince to spill the beans and dirty secrets. None! The newspaper maintains an anonymous email through our company URL that is used strictly for the purpose of protecting identities. I'll have no problems using this to reach the unsavory people and obtain your new identity and documents."

---

Once Sarah learned of Stephen's predicament, she was well prepared for his arrival and asked for a few days off claiming a family member was arriving in Kampala. Sarah was working in a city about two hours away called Jinja.

Max had gotten Stephen a new identity under the name Robert Hall. Max laughed as it was an old retail store in the US that had long ago gone out of business. On two levels he knew it was a good cover. First, the European guy creating the documents had no idea about the joke. Second, the name was totally common. Max returned to the apartment with the papers and told Stephen there was a reservation in his name with Lufthansa airlines for the next morning. He scheduled the flight for 6:00 AM hoping if Stephen had a tail, he'd be safer with an early morning flight. With less travelers in the airport it would be easier for Stephen to see if someone was following. Max's experience told him that when government clandestine operators were covering airports, shifts changed usually at 12-hour intervals. Logic and experience indicated that anyone watching the airport and train stations would have a changing of the guard around 6:00 AM.

Stephen and Max sat down to dinner with some Indonesian food Max had brought home. Max brought a bag over to the table and opened it, pulling out a few bottles of makeup and a wig. Stephen laughed.

Max laughed too. "Hey mate, this is serious. We've covered lots of bases here; documents, encrypted emails to Sarah, and we've selected the right time to take off given security shift changes. We don't know who's watching but we do know there will be lots of CCTV cameras at the airport. This disguise is a must, and we'll need to be up by 3:00 AM."

After dinner Max took out the makeup. He had plastic prostheses for the nose and the chin. He showed Max how this would work with elastic putty after which he would apply makeup foundation to blend the nose and chin into a solid base color. After they finished the overview of the disguise, they each took a shot of Vodka and went to bed.

The alarm went off at 3:00 and they bumped into each other as they entered the kitchen. They rubbed their eyes.

"This is it Mate," Max said, "let's get you suited up." After applying the prostheses and makeup, Max put the wig on Stephen's head and turned him to the mirror. "Perfect."

Max had rented a car the day before and had it in the alleyway behind his apartment block. His own car sat on the street in front of the apartment in case they might be watching the apartment. At 4:00 AM they sneaked out the rear of the apartment complex and got into the rental car. Stephen stayed on the floor in the back as a precaution. Upon arrival at the airport, Max drove to the rental car return and dropped the car. Max shook hands with Stephen, who smiled nervously and embraced him.

Max handed him the ticket. "Sarah will send me an email once she has met you in Kampala. Good luck," He turned and proceeded to the bus stop where airport employees got rides back to the city.

Stephen took a shuttle bus to the terminal. He got off with the other auto renters and proceeded to the immigration area. It was quiet. He hoped that if anyone was there watching, that the disguise would succeed. Stephen went through immigration without a hitch and it seemed no one was watching that he could tell. He boarded the plane, found his seat and waited for the jet to taxi. As it lifted off, he finally relaxed and closed his eyes for the nine plus hours to Uganda.

When the plane touched down in Uganda, Stephen noticed an old terminal riddled with machine gun pock marks and thought it strange. The he remembered this was where Idi Amin had held the Air France Jewish hostages on behalf of the Palestinian terrorists. He also recalled how the Israeli a surprise attack had overtaken the terrorists and freed all of the hostages. As the plane rolled past the old terminal, he saw coming into view the new Terminal, with a grand sign saying, *Welcome to Uganda*.

Stephen deplaned and went through immigration and finally customs. As he exited the secure area he finally saw Sarah. The smile on his face could only be matched by Sarah's. They embraced with a hug that surely lasted more than a full minute. They then stared at each other at arm's length for another few seconds.

Sarah grabbed his carry bag. "Let's get out of here. My car is just outside." Once inside the car Sarah stopped and they kissed again for a long moment. "My God, how I was worried. I got the details through Max's encrypted email."

"You know you have fallen in love with a criminal."

She laughed. "Well seeing as you're not a killer, based on what I know from Max, you were just doing what you thought was industrial espionage. Hey, I mean they make movies about that these days."

Stephen was embarrassed about his current issue, but he had no doubt Sarah also now knew about his former life, including his failed marriage and lost career. As she pulled out of the car park, there was silence for a minute.

Stephen turned to her. "So given all you know now, you are still in love with me?"

"More than ever guy. You were simply seeking a way out from where you were. True it was not what you had expected, but it's not hard to understand how a $1,000,000 offer to simply remap a DNA gene was an enticing lure given your situation. Look, I get where you were. Life seemed without hope and you took a leap. Yes, it was a bad leap, but can anyone say industrial espionage is evil? I certainly can't! I still love you and want us to spend our lives together once I am done here. I'm hoping you're of the same mind. For now, however we have bigger fish to fry. I've gotten a week off from the NGO in Jinja and have rented us an apartment here in Kampala. Let's get there now and get ourselves settled. I've got internet service in the apartment and my laptop is there. Once we get settled, we'll reach back to Max to see what he has learned about your situation."

Once they got back to the apartment, he dropped his bag, grabbed her by the waist, and they engaged in a long kiss.

"Let's get that awful disguise off," she said. After two rounds of makeup remover in the bathroom mirror, they exited with Stephen feeling—and looking like a new man. Sarah nodded at her handiwork. "Are you hungry?"

Without words, he took her hand and led her to the bedroom where they reengaged passionately. At first, they slowly undressed each other while their lips were inseparable, but within moments, they feverishly ripped off the rest of their clothing. They were like hungry animals who hadn't eaten for weeks, he on top of her until they each with exhaustion climaxed. From there they laid naked and fell arm and arm into a deep sleep.

They slept in, and later Sarah began pulling food out of the refrigerator. "I wasn't sure what your favorite dinner was but somehow I thought some fresh lamp chops might work."

Stephen laughed. "What are the chances you would know lamp chops are my favorite?"

"There's wine in the cupboard."

He shifted a few bottles around. "Ah a cab, this'll work."

He found a corkscrew and proceeded to open it. They shared a short toast.

"Let me get the chops into the broiler and then let's get the table settled."

The lamp chops were fabulous as was the wine. Surely, they found the food and drink minor players to the reality of their being together. After dinner they got down to Stephen's predicament.

"I feel you will be safe here in Uganda for the time being," Sarah said, "but sooner or later this situation must be resolved." She pulled out of her large knapsack a bunch of papers. "This was all sent to me by Max this morning. It's the best he was able to put together about your circumstances."

Sarah handed him three pages from Max's emails. Stephen began to read:

> Stephen, the information within this email is all I've been able to access through my channels. Suffice it to say I expect to have a lot more in the days to come. Through various bank channels I've been able to determine the fund backing the fake companies. While they were in many instances three or four steps removed, in the business of journalism, we have our sources.
>
> It seems there is a holding company controlled by six individuals. These individuals come from long established European families who each had family stakes in Africa prior to the freedom movements that began in the early 60s. The names were eventually found through Deutsche Bank, one of the oldest in Europe. From kings to

queens to international bankers, most everyone at some time has had an account with them.

This group of men I've found all had significant family wealth lost during the African continent's revolution to remove colonial powers. It seems that if devastation came to Africa through the HIV epidemic, these families would benefit through reclaiming factories and mines which were taken by the new freedom governments. They permitted these families to operate their former facilities as long as the government owned 51% of the entities.

You can only imagine the racist thoughts that were fomented when people of privilege had their assets stolen from them under the guise of legitimacy. Then they are told to continue running the operations only to give the lion share of profits up.

It seems rumors have been circulating that there is a contaminated shipment of the new HIV vaccine to be landed in Africa. As of my brief investigation, it seems no one knows for sure if this is true and they are retesting the vaccine. I am expecting more information tomorrow from a contact I have at a WHO lab as to the results of these tests. What is clear and evident is you have been singled out as the person who contaminated the vaccine. It's very early for much more information, but it seems clear that rumors are spreading about an out of work biotech PhD specialist, without giving him a name, who is involved in the contamination. They're searching for you worldwide.

I'm not sure how they planted this but it's almost like the Anthrax scare of 2001. Western governments have all been alerted and you are truly a wanted man. A bit of levity, I know you always wanted to be "the man" when we were in school, but today you truly are "the man." Stay safe and more information will follow. Given the circumstances, at least your best friend is on the inside and in your corner.

*Max*

After Stephen put down the sheets of emails, his face was truly ashen. Beyond killers, it seemed the men had quite a propaganda machine and had spread the word about him.

*Whether their people get to me or not, there can be no doubt I'm in as much trouble as is possible.*

# CHAPTER 14
## *Where to Turn*

Two days passed in Uganda. While Sarah and Stephen were enjoying being together, the reason for him being there was far from a holiday. It was constant stress and nerves simply sitting and waiting. Sarah could do little to keep tensions low, but she did her best by talking about what they would do once this crisis was over. It was 5:00 PM when her laptop dinged an incoming mail notification. Sarah started a different browser to see the private email she had set up via directions from Max.

The day before no emails came in except Max telling them to hold tight, and that he was still waiting for the WHO lab testing the vaccine. With dread and nervous anticipation Sarah clicked on the email message and then printed it out so they could stay offline. Max had said there would be phishing attempts to follow whoever he was in communication with from work. He felt it was always best to keep the computer offline, not open to a web browser.

*Stephen, this conspiracy is bringing out my own paranoia. I am trusting no one, not even friends at De Telegraafe. There's not much to say beyond the WHO has confirmed that the vaccine tested is functional without exceptions, no issues. Governments in Europe, the US and Africa are now breathing a sigh of relief and are preparing to commence releasing the vaccine by the end of this month (20 days). I'll be back to you as I learn more on the situation but in the*

73

meantime, people are looking for you—Interpol, the US CIA and others if you know what I mean. So, keep your head down and be safe (yeah that's you and my baby sister, lol).

Max

Having read this Stephen explained to Sarah that the DNA sequence he installed would not show or give negative results. The results will only change given human body temperature at 98.6 degrees Fahrenheit and that will only happen when the vaccine is injected into the human body. Prior to that its storage conditions are at 2 to 8 degrees Celsius. Under those conditions it is impossible to detect the toxic gene sequence prior to a temperature change.

"Oh my god, what do we do?" Sarah asked.

He wrote back to Max and explained that the results at the WHO prove nothing. He was quite sure that the DNA sequence he spliced into the vaccine, now being cloned in the billions, has the trigger where once the sequence is injected, the temperature change will alter it and the vaccine will become toxic.

Stephen turned to Sarah. "We must find a way to alert the WHO."

He composed a second email to Max and said we must get to the WHO ASAP. They waited for an answer from Max. Within minutes, Max wrote back and said

*Stephen you're being hunted. Check online, check news sources, check everywhere. Its as if you were the anthrax mailer of 2001. It's almost as if the Western nations want to insure you are found and put away in some dark corner to be prosecuted if even by the death penalty. It's as if they're making you out to be some mad racist scientist who wanted to cleanse the earth of inferior races forever. Truth be told Stephen, there are rumors panicking the world that you have contaminated numerous vaccines used in Africa and other parts of the world. Stay low and I'll get back to you.*

*Max*

"I'm getting extremely nervous here Sarah. It's almost as if this clandestine group, Ziff GMBH is spreading rumors about me which are the reality of *this group*. They're the racists wanting to kill off all the blacks in Africa to retake their former property. I'm the shill! After failing to kill me as they did with the others on the team, their next move is to poison the well and make me the person who has committed this heinous crime. It's what they had planned all along, only I screwed up their plan when they missed killing me.

"Their plan was in fact to kill off a massive portion of Africans given how large the HIV epidemic is. They knew the African leaders would insist on being the first inoculated. Now it appears through propaganda and the right government contacts, a clandestine group within these governments are behind this plan. They want me buried so they too can inherit Africa.

"Sarah, think about it. Who stands to gain the most if independent African nations fall? The Western Nations, the US, and the EU! The West is being diverted and falling right into the trap laid by these racists, whoever they are at Ziff GMBH. At this point the Chinese have been buying up Africa with loans. It's only a matter of time before China owns Africa and the West gets shut out from all the wealth and resources of Africa."

Sarah reeled from the onslaught of thoughts. "Wow, that's a huge chunk of fantasy to swallow."

"No, it's logical. Think about it. Elite Europeans divided up the middle east after first world war. Some say it was no different than Dick Cheney who wanted Iraq's oil and ensured the war would ensue using false information about WMDs, all planted by his personnel. Really think about it, it's all plausible." Stephen waited a moment for it all to sink in. "But where to go now?"

"I suppose all we can do is wait for Max to get more information. However, in the meantime, as I'm working for this NGO and we deal with infectious diseases, perhaps I can find someone pure enough to believe our supposition. Okay, let me make some calls."

# CHAPTER 15
## *On the Run*

Two more days passed without hearing from Max. Sarah and Stephen we're feeling more and more enclosed. Going out, even to the market, had become an adventure of disguises. They only ventured at midday, when the streets were mobbed, and the sun was high. High enough to make the heat such that even if spies lurked about, they would be forced to retreat every so often to seek shelter. Certainly, a more limited vantage point for looking out upon the sun baked streets.

While they were certainly happy being together, only three days remained before Sarah had to return to Jinga and leave Stephen alone in the small place she'd rented.

"How do we reach the WHO and other authorities," Stephen pondered, "ones who have not been blindsided by propaganda about me?"

How could he meet without fear of being set up? Even if he did it remotely by phone, given the current technologies, he could easily be tracked down to whereever he was. The only solution he could come to was using a trusted intermediary, a friend, but one with the gravitas to reach a major player at the WHO and get him to listen.

Sarah was doing whatever she could to be a sounding board for Stephen's thoughts. "Go back and think of the companies you've worked with. Were there any good friendships that know you well enough to never imagine you as a racist or a terrorist." She pressed him. "Stephen, think!"

He recalled Alphagene and before that Immunogen. He even considered old roommates from before his marriage. Inspiration struck on that point.Y

"Yes, Alfred! How I had forgotten Alfred Heinz?" He'd met Alfred through a want ad seeking a roommate. "If I can find Alfred, maybe I can use him as a conduit."

"Is he a bio geneticist?"

"No, he was a finance guy at a private investment bank. It's been 20 years. We were roommates, we lived together."

"Well, aren't roommates usually those that build the strongest bonds?" Hope filled Sarah's countenance.

"Yes and no, but it is true Alfred and I become very tight bro's, truly good friends who shared deep feelings. We lost touch after I met my wife. Yes, he was at the wedding ceremony, but we worked in such different fields. Once I was relocated by the firm to the west coast, we both found less and less time to be in contact. It's not hard to see how as life moved forward for both of us and we lost touch."

Sarah titled her head. "Stephen, even if we could locate Alfred, and he was more than happy to vouch for your character, how does that help us reach someone of scientific credibility the WHO would listen too?"

What Alfred did for a living back then was work with a firm that dealt with the health care sector. Stephen's thinking jumped two steps ahead as it was possible Alfred had contacts that could be high ranking leaders in the health care industry.

"Alfred Heinz was young private investment banker with big dreams of fortune, fame and was a good family man," Stephen said. "Often, he spoke of his desire to make it the clean way, marry and raise a family. He was a solid citizen. I know this to be true because at dinners when we were roommates, he often spoke of the unscrupulous ways Wall Street operated and he was determined to prove one could be a success with scruples. He was always raising capital for start-up companies as an investment banker. Who knows, perhaps one of those companies may well be a huge health care conglomerate now. I've no doubt Alfred has become a huge success wherever he landed.

"Do you know where he is these days."

"No, but hey there's always Google. Let's take a look and see if he's online. If we can locate him, maybe he'll have a direct contact with someone that could help us, or if nothing else, he can possibly lead us to someone well-placed to be an intermediary."

They went online to Google and typed in Alfred Thomas Heinz, and voila, there he was at Heinz, Morgan, Stratham. A little digging and it was clear Heinz, Morgan, Stratham was a huge Venture Capital bank focused on the Health Care Industry. The company's equity base was more than 5 billion.

Stephen smiled. "Like I said, I had no doubt Alfred would be 'a someone' one day, but I never thought he would be among the top three private equity banks in America."

They found a general information email but of course there was nothing listed for Alfred, however this was of little consequence, as Stephen felt that comfortable that if he wrote through the general contact info" email, that Alfred would recognize his name and reach out to him. Stephen immediately went to a local service provider in Uganda and set up a new email account and began composing.

*Subject: To the attention of Alfred Heinz*

*To whom it may concern, I am a very old friend of Alfred Heinz's. My name is Stephen Kennedy. I am currently overseas without an ability to communicate directly but it is of the utmost importance you bring to this email to Alfred's Heinz's attention.*

*Alfred old buddy, I know it's been a long time but I'm in a crisis and there is no friend who knows me better than you, despite the time and distance that has passed. I desperately need to communicate with you immediately in a matter of life or death. Please email direct to SMK@MNT.co.za*

# CHAPTER 16
## *The Intermediary*

As Africa was going to sleep, so New York was getting up for the work day. Alfred Heinz lived on the upper West Side with New York city's wealthiest, on Central Park West. Life had gone as planned. He was successful, and it was accomplished with honesty and scruples, as Alfred had promised to himself. He was now 44, married, with two boys, and a most admired individual through his benefits to society via the worldwide health care companies he served.

Initially, while he was raising Capital, he found a small company with technology that had tremendous applications for newborns with congenital organ failure. While they had raised a significant amount of capital, regulatory issues held back the company and it became increasingly difficult to convince investors to stay with the ship and its technology. Alfred regarded this technology highly while others walked away. He personally got involved using his own funds. Yes, it was tight for the next 36 months, but when the company finally received FDA approval, their technology to save newborns with deficient organ development was a tremendous success, and Alfred made his fortune.

It was 9:00 am and Alfred had just arrived at his office. Numerous people nodded their acknowledgment as he proceeded towards his corner office. Before it sat his secretary.

She stood. "Mr. Heinz, I can't be sure if this is a prank or what, but this email was sitting in the general information box for Heinz, Morgan, Stratham this morning. She presented the email print out to Alfred and he read it.

> Subject: To the attention of Alfred Heinz
>
> To whom it may concern, I am a very old friend of Alfred Heinz's. My name Stephen Kennedy. I am currently overseas without an ability to communicate directly but it is of the utmost importance you bring to this email to Alfred's Heinz's attention.
>
> Alfred old buddy, I know it's been a long time but I'm in a crisis and there is no friend who knows me better than you, despite the time and distance that has past. I desperately need to communicate with you immediately in a matter of life or death. Please email direct to SMK@MNT.co.za
>
> Stephen Kennedy

Alfred stood frozen for a moment. It wasn't as if he didn't recognize the name, but it was the message therein; "life or death." Could anything grab you harder?

His secretary saw the look on his face. "Sir, is this for real?"

"I'm not sure what's real and what is not, but I do know Stephen Kennedy very well and these words certainly garnered my concerns."

"Is there was anything I can do?"

But Alfred was already turning to his office. "No."

He began to type on his desk top computer. He entered the specified email address.

> My gosh, its been year. I can't imagine what Stephen could be involved in to use the words "life or death."
>
> Dear Stephen, to say hearing from you was a surprise is an understatement but to read the words life or death, is absolutely frightening. I wish we could speak now but I take it from your cryptic email that communication directly has its perils and I'll defer to your reply as to how or when we can speak directly. My direct email

is *Aheinz@HMS.com. I await your reply and pray I may be of true help if your situation is as dire as you imply.*

*Your buddy,*

*Alfred*

As Alfred was writing to Stephen at 9:30 in the morning, it was already 3:30 pm in Kampala, Uganda. When the email came in, a wave of relief came over Stephen's soul. It was heartening that Alfred was so attentive as to write back so quickly and so resolutely.

Sarah was in the kitchen preparing dinner when Stephen called to her to read Alfred's email.

She smiled. "Well it's a start, and a darn good one."

Stephen and Sarah took a moment to sigh in relief. They thought about how they might explain it all in an email to Alfred. As the sun set, they decided to go to sleep early as the stress of being hunted had taken a toll.

The next morning only 48 hours remained before Sarah needed to return to Jinga. Stephen asked her about the NGO.

"Do they use satellite phones?"

"Yes," she replied. "But why?"

"Because they're tracking me, whether western governments or the group that has been trying to kill me. I need to talk to Alfred and a satellite phone is the only way we can be sure no one can hear the conversation between us. It will also keep anyone from finding me even if they're searching in Uganda!"

Rather than wait the 48 hours to return to her NGO in Jinga, she and Stephen got in her car and drove the two hours to get there.

"How are you going to explain to the site director," Sarah asked, "that you need to use the satellite phone?"

"There is no explaining. *You* are going to have to sneak into the base camp office and get it. Given the time zone difference, surely, we can wait for midnight for you to try."

"But what about you," Sarah pressed. "I'm sleeping in a dormitory of 12 workers. There's no way you can stay with me without raising eyebrows."

"Park the car at the edge of the village. I'll stay inside until you return with the SAT phone. Let me get behind the wheel and use your cell phone to message Alfred. Tell him you are my girlfriend and use the code phrase, *'no one screws up twice baked potatoes the way Alfred does!'* He'll remember that as it was a constant pain in his neck. They were always too loose because he used too much sour cream." They both laughed. "In your email tell Alfred I apologize but he needs to be ready to get a call from me at 6:00 AM on his cell. Oh, and BTW, make sure your email requests his cell number."

# CHAPTER 17
## S.O.S.

When they arrived in Jinga it was just after dark. Stephen parked within 100 meters of the village, but well hidden by a clump of trees. The NGO camp was set up in a clear savannah with lots of space for the clinics as well as a temporary helicopter pad. Sarah and David rested their heads against the seat backs and closed their eyes waiting for the camp to settle into a close for the evening. Around 11:30 they crept quietly toward the encampment. They watched and waited for another 20 minutes to insure all was quiet and everyone had turned in for the night. The communications tent was dark. Sarah had no doubt that the entire camp was in bed and, hopefully, sound asleep.

"We've got to go now, Sarah. Alfred is expecting my call in 10 minutes."

Sarah was shaking. Although hesitant, she knew there were no other options. For the first time in her life she was involved in an illicit affair. Of course, she knew and loved Stephen, but nevertheless it was a first at being a thief. Yes, the SAT phone would be returned afterwards, but Sarah had been a Pollyanna all of her life. The protected youngest.

She stealthy left the edge of the woods and in a low crouch got to the tent. She glanced about, then opened the door, went to the communications desk. She grabbed the satellite phone and almost tripped on her own steps as she fled quickly.

Returning to the edge of the woods where Stephen was waiting, she dropped to her knees and handed Stephen the phone. She giggled a bit, feeling the exhilaration of crossing a line she had never crossed before, something akin to theft, even if she would be replacing it in minutes. It was 12:03 AM and Stephen quickly dialed Alfred's cell number. The phone rang and Alfred answered. They exchanged only a few words of greeting before Alfred began.

"Let get right to the words, *life or death*. Pretty scary."

Stephen began by explaining the details of his life since last they saw each other. He spoke of his marriage, the divorce, the loss of work in late 2007 when the world's financial market went upside down. He further explained how the loss of the marriage and career caused a deep mental slump. By 2009 he felt there was little to live for. His work prospects had not improved, and he was desperate financially. Payments for alimony were high, as his wife had never worked. During their tine together she had been desperate for a child. She also started a home gift business that never took off.

"Perhaps her own failure in business," Stephen proposed, "and inability to have a child, led to the failed marriage. Whoever was to blame, I was broke and forlorn and answered an advert from Europe seeking a bio geneticist for a special project. The qualifications for the job required a single person without attachments and certainly that was who I had become. The job required a clandestine team on a commercial espionage mission to clone and steal a formula for the new HIV vaccine. To me, it was merely, even if I was kidding myself, typical behavior among the major pharmaceutical companies.

"Surely you must have heard yesterday the announcements on CNN, et al, and from the WHO." It was time for Stephen to explain the life or death part. "Alfred, on this so called commercial espionage job, I thought I was cloning this Transgene company's HIV vaccine sequence, but in fact I was inserting a puck, a change, if you will. I inserted a DNA sequence that will make the vaccine deadly to anyone receiving it within 30 days of inoculation."

"Oh My God!"

"Everyone who was on my team has been killed in non-conspicuous accidents," Stephen said. "I have been followed and they tried to kill me. From what I have been able to put together, the group that hired me uses as many as three or four shell companies to separate themselves from the people I interviewed with. In the end I'm being hunted and what's worst is we've got to stop those inoculations in Africa. Millions could die. I cannot stick my head up anywhere to try and reach anyone as my name is now poison. If you have not been following the news as of yesterday, they've coined me as the same type of crazy, out-of-work, radical terrorist as Bruce Edward Irvins. You remember, the microbiologist accused of the Anthrax mailings of 2003. Irvins at least had a job. They are painting me as a total loser."

"How can I be of help?" Alfred asked.

"I need an intermediary. Are you still in the healthcare sector?"

"More than you can imagine."

"I had hoped as much. There's no doubt the people behind this plot are racists and likely seeking to access the wealth of Africa by eradicating populations. This would allow their interests, whether governments or the private sector, to regain control of Africa before the Chinese end up owning it all. Obviously with a death contract on me, whether by my former employers, or now Western governments looking for me having been influenced by this unknown cartel, I'm a dead man if I stick my head up anywhere."

"Where the hell are you?"

Stephen filled him in briefly about Max and his sister Sarah but ended that part of the conversation. "Alfred, its better you and your family don't know where I am. These people are big league. Think about it. They are ready to eradicate an entire race of people in Africa. Getting rid of you and your family would be small potatoes. If in some way you become compromised, I've no doubt after witnessing the deaths of my teammates, they would not hesitate to come after you to get to me!"

"So where do we go from here?"

"Who do you know in the healthcare biotech arena that's notable and would be able to get the ear of someone in the HIV infectious disease section at the WHO? Someone they'd listen to."

Alfred thought for a moment. "I don't have any contacts in the infectious disease area, but I do have senior contacts within MSF (Medicines sans Frontiers) who are focused on prenatal health. It's been almost twenty years, so you wouldn't know, but I've left the venture capital world and put all of my money into a company that works on pre and perinatal cellular organ development. Hence my connection with Francois Duvalier at MSF. It's my main business now. I'd take the time to explain how I evolved into this health area but its irrelevant for the moment. What is relevant is I have the director of MSF as a close associate and I am confident we can seek his help."

"That's fabulous!" Stephen was exuberant at the bit of good news.

"How do we begin this rescue journey?"

"Let me prepare a full explanation and a DNA schematic to the extent I can on what I did in my work for this company called GRC (Genetics Resources Company) and Ziffer GMBH who ran the advert that sent me to them. While this conglomerate may be lost in the winding trail of shell companies, which may have all disappeared by now, perhaps after we are successful in halting the HIV vaccine inoculations, Interpol or other international agencies will get to searching out this private group. For now, we've millions to save. I will send a written explanation and a DNA schematic for you to forward to your friend at MSF. If your friend can get it to the right people, we should be able to stop this."

Stephen outlined how the vaccine stored is at 2° to 8° Celsius and it will not exhibit any of the toxic effects at those temperatures. "I'll explain how my DNA manipulation causes the toxicity to form. They can verify it once the vaccine is inoculated into humans or any animal that has a normal temperature range within a few degrees of a human. Using a micron microscope, the molecular changes in the vaccine will become apparent. Once the recombinase catalyzes the genetic material, any doctor or researcher worth their salt will see this."

They concluded the call, which had now gone more than 30 minutes. Sarah determined that despite the two hour drive, it was probably best they did not go to her dormitory bunk. While occasionally romantic partners had spent the night, she was sure the camp was as much as a rumor mill as any laundromat. Plus they had no idea if any of them kept up with the news. Surely Stephen's photo had been all over the media.

He agreed and they then drove back to Kampala arriving by 3:00 AM. When they arrived, knowing it was now just 9:00 AM in NYC, he began to work on composing the full story with as many details to which he had privilege. He included a DNA schematic of where he inserted the puck in the double helix chain and disclosed which restriction enzyme GGPT used to cleave the helix. It was around 5:00 AM when he finished and Sarah sent the email through a new email using the MNT browser, most common to the poor in Africa and probably the least scanned. True terrorists never use public email servers.

Knowing the email was sent and Alfred would be receiving at 11:00 AM EST, they fell to sleep on the bed, exhausted, arm in arm.

# CHAPTER 18
## *The Leak*

Alfred received the email and immediately asked his secretary to place a call to Francois Duvalier, director of Neonatal work for MSF in Geneva. The urgency in his voice along with the strange email that came into the general corporate contact address certainly piqued her interest. Mary had been his secretary for more than 7 years. She was loyal and also kept her eye on industry inside information that came through their press office.

She thought his urgent request to reach Dr. Duvalier out of his character, as he did not speak in his usual calm manner. She found the number and placed the call immediately. She observed him converse through the glass partition to his office. Alfred seemed very animated in a distressed manner. Her curiosity continued to be aroused.

The call ended and he came out.

"Is there anything else you need?" she asked. :I was going to head down the the break room for a coffee."

"No, that's fine." He waved her off.

Alfred had explained with exacting detail the information he got from Stephen. He explained to Francois that while it appears that Stephen is some kind of out of work radical terrorist, it was not true, but rather a smear campaign propagated by those who had organized this faux commercial espionage, which had gotten Stephen into this mess.

Alfred emphasized the timeline was critical and that perhaps only 20 days remained before the inoculation campaign would begin.

At first Francois was somewhat skeptical, but he also knew how far they'd come in the area of genetic cloning alteration for neonatal organs. Francois was aware of his company's history, how Wall Street investors abandoned them and how Alfred took all he had, including mortgaging his own home to bring their dreams to fruition. Francois had no other choice than to believe with all his spirit that every word Alfred had conveyed must be true!

When they hung up the phone Francois immediately called Dr. Genovese, the head of the World Health Organization. After a fifteen-minute phone discussion which did not necessarily go well, Dr. Genovese was for the most part in disbelief. While Genovese trusted and knew Dr. Duvalier very well from their work together on many committees in Geneva, the idea still seemed preposterous, given that they had all gone through the testing. In the end, Duvalier pressed as hard as he could to request that things be held up until a retesting of the vaccine could be accomplished.

"What harm can that cause?" Duvalier asked.

"Well better safe in this area than not," Genovese responded, "but there will be political consequences if we hold off. Pandora's box has been opened and the world's expectations of release this month has caused tremendous pressure on us should we delay, especially given the millions in Africa suffering from the disease. Nevertheless, I will hold everything up and begin a retest." Genovese let out a long breath. "Transgene had passed all three clinical trials. There will be a huge backlash on the WHO."

"Yes, but those tests were done prior to the scale up production," Duvalier said.

"But that's exactly when this group broke into the lab facility and rearranged the DNA sequence. *Post* all clinical trials, so no one would ever know the vaccine was toxic within 30 days once injected."

In the end Genovese agreed to put a hold on distribution and restart a new test with monkeys. If Duvalier's claims were true, this was at the safest genus to work with to see if this insane supposition could be true.

When Mary, Alfred's secretary entered the break lounge she saw Stuart Rose, the head of PR for Heinz, Morgan, Stratham. He was a sneaky guy in many ways. Mary always thought Stuart was a bit unctuous, always with a self-serving edge to him. She was cautious when they spoke. After all she was exposed to private information regularly as she was Alfred's personal assistant.

His job was to promote the company's image, and since the company was the major shareholder of HRC, he also handled the public relations for them. Mary greeted Stuart with a smile and poured herself a cup of coffee. Stuart always understood that he existed at the discretion of the board and they decided the direction of the PR, not Stuart. This was always a rub for him given his resume and experience. He was rarely, if ever, in the board meetings. Not until they invited him and described the direction they wanted to promote for HMS and HRC. He never felt like he was on the inside and he truly was not despite his thirty successful years in PR.

"So what's up at the big meeting today?" Stuart asked.

Mary looked up from pouring her coffee. "It's been postponed until the afternoon."

"Why?" He had seen Alfred arrive earlier than usual.

Mary tried to remain nonchalant. "Some phone call to Dr. Duvalier from MSF pushed everything back."

"So is MSF involved?" Stuart, true to form, was curious. "Could the WHO be influencing HRC?"

"I have no idea," Mary answered. "It was a private call and his door was shut. I saw him gesticulating and he had a concerned look on his face. I guess something was up, however I have no idea what."

They finished their conversation with some discussions about HRC's delivery of the new neonatal organ tissue cloning. Both agreed how much it would mean to the poor worldwide. Mary finished her coffee, bid adieu to Stuart, and returned to her desk.

Stuart returned to his office and went online to look for any information regarding HRCs competition. Part of being a great PR individual was always to stay abreast of current trends and market demands relevant to HRCs field. He could in turn translate this into corporate revenue, which would have a direct correlation on his position. Greater success meant greater budgets for PR events, a greater salary, bonuses, and a better lifestyle for Stuart!

The first thing he keyed into his computer was to find out what was going on at the WHO. He searched their web site for press releases. The WHO was certainly something he paid attention to regularly. After just a few minutes he saw an announcement citing that the HIV vaccine to be released at the end of the month was being delayed citing issues regarding distribution. Stuart thought this odd as it was unusual for the WHO to announce a date for the start of inoculations without having a firmed-up the supply chain.

The WHO was not just a medicine distribution organization, that was more in the realm of the UN through UNHR or UNICEF. A pull back at this juncture would have real consequences to its reputation and it would impact nation state donors who depend on the WHO as a global surveillance organization to fight infectious diseases. The WHO are the recognized gold standard for other nations to follow, especially since the onset of commercial jet transportation in the early 1960s, when air travel for the general population became accessible. Reality today was that anyone could board a plane and within 18 hours be anywhere. Contagions often took at least 24 to 48 hours to present symptoms. This technological transformation in travel was the main reason for the ascension of the WHO as the premier disease surveillance organization for the entire medical world.

Having read the press release, Stuart made a call to one of his inside lackeys whom he used frequently as a source of information. When he called his source and inquired about the delay, his source said that the word around the administration was the Dr. Genovese received a request from Dr. Duvalier to hold up the distribution date.

"Pas quoi?" Stuart loved the effect of using his French, which of course many inside the WHO spoke as their first tongue, being that it was located in Geneva. His contact could only relate that he heard from the infectious vaccine laboratory that there was a temperature stabilization issue.

Afterward, Stuart began a reconstruction of pipelines from the producer, Transgene, to the developer, to the production company producing the millions of doses until he arrived at the company responsible for the shipping and distribution of the vaccine. Nothing seemed out of the ordinary. Drawing a blank he went in any direction he could. Finally, after no new revelations, he pondered his next move.

Maybe some deep searches beginning at some porn sites might lead him into the dark web, and he would see what might be out there. He'd never done this before, but he saw adverts for mercenaries and that led to an entire area given to weapons and human recruitment for military type services. As he dug deeper it seemed many a real conspiracy, not theory, but real clandestine operations could be found beyond other contrivances. Surely most soldiers of fortune and mercenary types sought work through adverts on the dark web.

Once in this area, he entered the key words HIV VACCINE. The first thing which popped up was a story regarding a terrorist who was a bio-geneticist. It seemed that a number of private security agencies were searching for this guy and there was a hefty bounty for the disposal of this person, with a footnote citing a contact with the address of <u>programme@</u>

orange.de. Beyond that there also seemed to be government type postings from Western Nation state clandestine agencies.

*There must be something big going on here…*

These didn't seem to be standard CIA, FSB or ASIO, but deep state. More like the types that if it gets out, they disavow you—that is you disappear. It was like reading a fiction novel, but it seemed these people really exist. Based on what he was reading, they were obviously "the deep state," and they too wanted to erase a worldwide terrorist threat from the earth without making it public.

Stuart ruminated on all this information from the dark web combined with the WHO pull back. First, a bio-geneticist was wanted worldwide, yet it was not officially announced. When had the WHO ever made an announcement on the start of a program unless everything was in place? The hunt for the bio-genetic terrorist began almost exactly at the same time the WHO pulled back. They had to be connected! Given his deductions, it seemed clear that everyone was looking for the bio-geneticist.

Stuart was beginning to piece it all together. The connection was uncanny. Two weeks earlier the HIV vaccine was announced, then a week later, on the dark web, private agencies and clandestine governments want this person erased. Then a delay of distribution. It signified this bio-engineer terrorist had somehow impacted the vaccine to cause the WHO to halt distribution and retest the vaccine in its laboratory.

All that Stuart had put together, combined with learning from Mary that Alfred spoke with Duvalier early that morning, moved him to believe that the reason for Alfred Heinz's call to Dr. Duvalier on the same day that the WHO announced a delay in the HIV inoculation program was that the bio-terrorist being hunted did something to the vaccine. He quickly went online again to open a new fictitious email account with AOL. He always used Gmail, as he could get the most versatile professional features, even more than Yahoo. AOL and MSN were filled with lots of distracting, unwanted spam and news. Gmail was strictly for those focused on retrieving mail. As such it focused only on the most important features for a professional where mail was their main priority.

AOL, as the first URL, had lost most of its business to an aging population whereas newer URLs, like Yahoo, Firefox and Gmail, came in offering more cloud based services focused strictly on email. AOL's unwieldy platform made it difficult to innovate with so many facets from news, services and advertising running. It was a messy platform and not user friendly for corporations, but perfect for his purposes to be lumped into an aging population who would likely be the last people to be looked at if you were tracking who was responding to the posted address of programme@orange.de. He had a strong hunch having found this on the dark web. He was treading into an unknown area outside of his skill set.

He left the office and caught a taxi downtown near the west village to find an internet café. Internet cafes were becoming a thing of the past in business districts, as most anyone working in commercial enterprises had internet service. The west village was an area where many older people as well as out of work people were not able to have personal internet service in their homes. He also wanted to distance himself from his workplace in case someone was tracking him. He wasn't concerned about someone following him but rather the tracking of the location of his internet point of access.

It was a miserable day. The rain was incessant, and one needed more than simply a raincoat. So he changed out of his Johnston & Murphy's into a pair of old loafers kept under his desk shoes for days just like this. By the time he walked into the Café his suit was soaked despite wearing his heavy trench coat. He wiped away the rain from his forehead with his handkerchief while presenting his credit card to be assigned a computer. It was an older internet café where you could not simply swipe your credit card. He sent an email to programme@orange.de and sat for a moment, waiting for a reply. What came back shook his core and scared him enough to realize this was not a good direction. He shut down the internet café computer and rushed back to his office.

At his office he opened his computer and returned to the dark web. At a certain level he was excited but, on another level, while he stayed with his investigation, he wanted distance and anonymity. If people were seeking to kill someone then this could be a dangerous situation for him. Being even remotely connected could spell real danger. Real clandestine people could be ruthless. He wanted to insure he was not collateral damage for the secrets he had discovered and put together from the dark web. Stuart proceeded, feeling somewhat distant from things, as he did not answer the reply. He was also confident that his new AOL account used at a internet café could not be traced back to him.

In following through on his deductive reasoning, only a few scenarios could explain why a PhD bio-geneticist would go rogue. He had an idea and began searching pharmaceutical companies and layoffs during the crash of September 2007. He figured a bio-geneticist might go rogue because he's looney, or because he lost his. Financial pressure could force people into many bad choices. Who knew where anger and debt could lead?

He compiled lists of more than 1200 laid off bio-geneticists from the top 20 pharma companies involved in vaccine research. Stuart was a very bright individual. After compiling this list, which told him very little, he decided he needed some AI, so he contacted a professor he knew at a leading university who was a statistician. Stuart asked him about software programs where he might be able to correlate various indicators against a postulate to create a probable correlation eliminating those that don't fit the postulate.

"Sure you could do a regression analysis whereby you enter X number of variables to eliminate what doesn't fit your postulate," his friend said. "Your regression line will show you the best fit based on the variables you've identified. You can get some programs online that will do this for as cheap as $39.99."

He bought the software and loaded the 1200 laid off researchers. Using court records he determined who owed debts in combination with divorces within the last year. It seemed those were two logical factors that might drive a PhD bio-geneticist to go rogue. Losing everything and seeking to make money was easier to determine than simply being a looney.

After a few minutes the name of Stephen Kennedy arose with the highest probability of being the bio-geneticist sought for erasure from this earth! He went out to a different internet café and wrote to programme@oranmge.de saying he knew who the bio terrorist was and left for the day with a smile that he had figured out the puzzle. Surely there was a possibility of financial reward for the information he deduced.

The next day Stuart didn't show up for work, because Stuart never woke.

# CHAPTER 19
# *Group of Six Vanishes*

Two days after the WHO delayed the distribution of the HIV vaccine, Roger Atwell received an early morning call from Nigel Jones.

"Roger, we've yet to locate our missing piece." It was a code phrase they liked to use for the last person yet to be eliminated from their project. It was ever the concern that someone might be listening in on any conversation. "Unfortunately, we have larger problems. A fishing line looking to catch our missing piece on the dark web got a bite. However, the bite wasn't from our missing person, but from someone who deduced his real name."

"I suppose this does pose more than a wrinkle," Roger agreed.

"If this bite found out who he was, there's a possibility that the piece's name might have already gotten out, and eventually expose the Group of Six. Of course we dealth with this loose bite immediately, and they're no longer a threat."

"Well that's just grand," Roger said. "Look, whoever is keeping our missing piece hidden surely offers us an opportunity to find him. Regardless of what our piece said about being single and unattached, he had to have had a previous life. Whoever is assisting him must be traceable through family, friendships or previous working associates."

"We could ultimately find them, but it doesn't aid our plan. His elimination no longer is of value. Somehow he has gotten to someone and our toxic vaccine is being retested!" Nigel was more concerned than he had ever been during the project. "Have you looked online or read a morning paper"?

"My good man," Roger retorted in classic British fashion, "I've just been awoken by you sir. What have I missed?"

He told Roger about the WHO press release stating they were delaying the start of the HIV vaccine inoculation for supply chain distribution issues. "Something has spooked them. They're retesting and will find out about the temperature activation. Then they'll do a challenge test and inject live specimens. At that point within 30 days the test subjects will go into a toxic state. The phony documents will be reviewed, and they will expose the transposition of the DNA sequence and the grand plan is shot."

"Alright, maybe its bullocks for us, but how does it get back to the Group?" Roger asked.

"Once they announce they're withdrawing the vaccine, our missing piece will realize he's safe and turn himself in. Our planned African genocide will never materialize. He'll be protected by the media. As of now, he's a crack pot, but once the WHO announces their findings, he'll come out and work with the authorities. They won't harm him. They need him, Jail would be preferable to a death sentence from us. He'll receive some, but being an unwitting participant and his ensuing assistance will minimize it to little or none. He will become the key to uncovering the plot and who we are. We've no choice but to call an immediate meeting of the Group to make proactive decisions for our own protection."

Encrypted emails were sent out after the call by Nigel and the group of Six met the next morning. They all sat down and the senior staff aide to Herr Dressler closed the thick wooden doors. The meeting began with Nigel giving the details of what had transpired.

"Ultimately it won't be hard to seek out who would have gained the most. Since we enlisted the aid of clandestine western government agencies we are at the core of the hunt for our missing piece."

"But they were complicit with us too," Fredrick said. "They were willing to go along to retrieve the rich resources of Africa before the Chinese usurped them via their un-payable infrastructure loans. We're look at twenty nations that could fall."

"While one might think they were complicit, in this scenario numbers work against us." Nigel said. "We're not talking about a cabal of merely a dozen. There may be one hundred or more people just between the US and Europe. Too many people who knew what was going to take place, *the genocide* which we initiated. They we will stay silent and protect their nation's reputations. How would it look to the world if certain nations were exposed to have gone along with the idea of killing blacks in Africa through a toxic HIV vaccine in order to prevent China from continuing the takeover. *We* will be slated as the designers of the Genocide. The West, however, was merely trying to catch a terrorist, as they will play it before the world's media. They will all be very aware that a scandal could erupt, and they will prevent any association by shredding every document, deleting emails, erasing correspondence, wiping hard drives, texts, even disavowing personnel. There will be no loyalty to our Group, short of money. But while money may have been a possible solution to the higher ups inside, there are always boy scouts, the do-gooders amidst those in their ranks. No, money can't be guaranteed to silence everyone. That gentlemen, is an extremely dangerous course of action I can guarantee we will lose. We must accept the plan has been foiled, no matter how we thought it was impregnable, and move to a proactive position immediately. Otherwise, we will be lucky to be exiled like Napoleon, living in our Elba wherever that might be, never to see the light of day."

"We must all immediately liquidate assets and terminate subsidiaries," Nigel said. "Yes, we will lose our holdings in Africa, but we are all still very wealthy men. Would anyone dispute that even with one hundred million or so, given our current estates, that we couldn't survive? Please gentlemen, let us all be realists. We are a greedy lot but better to escape prosecution when compared to a life sentence in prison."

"How would it not be trackable back to us," Fritz Kronner asked, "even if we relinquish our shares in the African subsidiaries?"

Nigel addressed the Group, not just Fritz. "Greed, gentlemen, is at the cornerstone of those in power in those nations. We can all rest assured that each of our assets when abandoned will be welcomed, literally unnoticed by the rest of the rest of the world and be kept quiet. The leaders of these African nations which we were about to destroy are as derelict as any pieces of our plot since rising to power. From Zimbabwe to Uganda to Kenya to Angola to the DRC, their elections are figments of the populace's imagination. Yes, maybe one day they will be overthrown, but not in our lifetimes. Corrupt leaders who've stolen the wealth from their nations and their cronies will gladly embrace the rest of our shares quietly. If they were overthrown in a decade or even less, who would believe a Mugabe, who has billions in the bank, or any of them? They'd be running for their lives. They will keep all the assets we relinquish, all for themselves. There would never be any public disclosure. Its laughable to think any of them would have a thought to create a public company for sharing the wealth with their people.

"No, we're safe within their greed. It's the one thing we can count on in the world. If any of you doubt my assumption, take a look in the mirror at yourselves. Would you give away your fortunes to the poor? Let us not pretend the world is any different than we know it to be. There will be no need to implicate us as to why we are yielding our share, short of us saying we've decided we are giving back to Africa. Even the Western powers had a singular focus, acquiring the wealth and resources of Africa and blocking the growth of China's beachhead.

"Gentlemen the world is greedy, and nations act in their individual self-interests. Yes, our wealth going forward we will be curtailed, but the greed of the same Africa leaders we sought to eliminate will ensure they continue going forward, cheating their people, removing us from suspicion, let alone prosecution. I've no doubt the WHO's reputation and that of the pharmaceutical companies will keep this quiet as well. There will be another vaccine one day minus whatever shortfall they pin on this one. We will all be somewhat less wealthy by some margin, but we will be free men, not languishing in prison. Gentlemen if any of you think there is another way, I welcome hearing it, but short of this plan, if we are found out, none of us will ever see the light of day."

# CHAPTER 20
## *Into the Light of Day*

The WHO lab finished its testing of seventy Resus monkeys. The test split inoculations between placebo saline and actual vaccine. The concentrations were amplified to accelerate the intensity, as well was to assure a rapid secure binding of sequences. Plus, the incubation temperature was set at 45 degrees C. It was only 3 days before Dr. Genovese was able to conclusively announce there was a problem with the vaccine and there would be a delay. The results confirmed what Dr. Duvalier had indicated.

Dr. Genovese closed the lab folder and glanced out his window. The results did not need a second glance. While Genovese had been concerned by Duvalier's call, he still hoped it wasn't the truth. Funny how it was a bright and a sunny day when he was handed the lab results. Yet everything seemed to turn dark once reading them. His corner office received plenty of sunlight, so much that the glare often forced him to pull down the shades. He looked out his window and thought to himself, how does such a beautiful day turn in one instant by opening a folder. He was a scientist and understood that in the blink of an eye, data could change everything. Life in so many ways as a scientist was binary. It goes from zeros to ones or back without reservation.

Once the WHO had had enough time to meet with senior staff to prepare for this extremely negative announcement, he had his secretary call for a press conference. After that he called Duvalier to say he was right and indeed the data confirms the vaccine will turn toxic in approximately 25 to 35 days.

Duvalier breathed heavily that Alfred's information was accurate. "There were so many people in Africa counting on this vaccine, and now their dreams are dashed. So many nations and, so many people within those countries will be devastated." The silence was deafening on both ends of the phone. "So, when will you make the announcement?"

"Tomorrow," Genovese said, "that's the soonest we can bring the major press organizations in. It's not just CNN. We must ensure all press groups are here for the announcement, particularly Al Jazeera, as they cater to audiences in much of the northern half of Africa."

"Is there anything I can do?"

"No," Genovese replied. "My secretary will handle all arrangements."

Soon after that call ended, an equally somber one occurred between Duvalier and Alfred. After hanging up Alfred immediately typed a message to a clandestine email address set up for Stephen.

*Stephen all you claimed has been validated over a three-day stress test using Resus monkeys at a 45 degree C with an eight-fold concentration titer. Regardless of the consequences you need to come into the light. Unquestionably the next step is to assist the authorities in tracking down those responsible for this tragedy. Stephen, trust me, I will be your front man until we can get assurances from the various agencies that you will be kept safe and treated with fairness. You were an unwitting participant and had no idea what this was about. I've arranged for an MSF helicopter to fly into the NGO camp to ferry you and Sarah back to Kampala to catch a commercial flight to Amsterdam. You'll use your fake doc's you got from Max. Hex will arrange for the authorities to get to you before those hunting you can. Looking forward to your reply,*

## Your friend Alfred

It had been three days since Stephen last communicated with Alfred. He was, as some would say, sitting on needle—which in his case was a Rondavel, an African style thatched cylinder in the bush waiting for Sarah to arrive. It was a steamy day, as was common in the bush where the humidity was almost at 100% and the clouds just shy of sitting on the ground. It was difficult not constantly wipe the salty sweat from your brow before it stung your eyes.

Despite what would be waiting for him when he returned to the world, he was quite tired of hiding, especially given current conditions. Nevertheless, he had Sarah, a love he never thought to recapture, and with him they were going to make things right. Sarah only had one more day until her six-month assignment was completed. Since arriving back in Jinga, Sarah couldn't risk letting him stay in her dormitory, given there were other NGO workers sharing the space and she had no idea how aware they were of the manhunt for Stephen. While there was no TV to watch any news, still most all had laptops and she had no doubt at minimum, in passing, they were aware of the worldwide hunt for the bio terrorist Stephen Kennedy.

She found an old safari lodge, long since out of business. The caretaker was someone far from having access to a TV or a laptop. She had arranged for Stephen to be able to stay for the final three days until she was free of her commitment. It was abandoned, but she was able to get two of the native workers to clean it up sufficiently for Stephen. As tomorrow was Sarah's last day, she had already made plans with the NGO director to catch a lift on the weekly supply plane landing tomorrow at the local air strip. Far from any kind of airport, it was enough for a DC-3 cargo plane to ferry in provisions and even ferry out a critically ill patients which could not be handled at the missionary hospital in the bush. The supply plane would transport her and Stephen to Kampala where she could catch a commercial airliner to head back to Europe.

"But what about the helicopter from MSF Alfred arranged for us?" Stephen asked.

"I'm concerned, and you should be too," Sarah chided, "not about Alfred but that he was the one who contacted the WHOI. If there are any inside the WHO that aree part of the plot, it could be dangerous getting on the MSF helicopter. Better we get to Max without anyone knowing what we are doing. By the time we get there, Max will have gotten to the authorities and Interpol, and we can at least feel somewhat protected."

"I suppose I agree. I don't doubt Alfred's loyalty, but we really don't know who is at the WHO."

"It'll be a slippery maneuver, but I'm going to distract the supply plane pilot while you sneak onboard."

She had made friends with the pilot before when she used the supply plane to get to Kampala to meet Stephen. Ordinarily she would have announced him as many natives and missionary workers ferried back and forth to Kampala weekly for family visits or personal supplies, but she was quite fearful, and it was best to keep him a secret.

In the morning Sarah used one of the compound's carpool jeeps to fetch Stephen and brought him to the air strip. He waited off to the side as the entire area was busy with workers taking cargo off the plane and boarding local workers for the return trip. As the pilot went into the flight shed to use the bathroom, Sarah, ran to the bushes alongside the air strip and grabbed Stephen and almost dragged him to the plane. He got into the back and hid behind some cargo crates and sat quietly. When Sarah returned, she peered toward the rear cargo, saw Stephen and held a finger to her mouth communicating a *shhhh!* The turnaround time on these landings was never more than 30 minutes. A simple unload of cargo and reload of personnel heading back to Kampala.

They arrived without incident at a private small airfield. They caught a taxi to Entebbe International. It was only a 25-minute ride along the Entebbe Expressway, a gift to Uganda through loans by the Chinese. The expressway felt almost as if you were in Europe or America. When they arrived, they went to the KLM counter to inquire about the next direct flight to Amsterdam. By now it was just before 3:00 PM and to their surprise there was a night flight at 11:00 PM direct to Amsterdam.

They bought their tickets with Sarah's credit card. Stephen presented his counterfeit documents and there were no questions but of course the real test was when they went through immigration for departure. They did what everyone does for a night flight, hunker down, drink lots of coffee, and take naps. Sitting on a bench they talked about the future once this nightmare was over.

"Are kids in the equation?" Sarah asked.

Stephen laughed. "Are you kidding? Of course, we'll make beautiful children."

At 8:30 the flight was opened and the two of them headed towards the immigration departure area. Stephen was a bit nervous but thought if the docs got him there, then they should be good enough to get him back. At the immigration queue Sarah went first. The officer asked what she had been in Uganda for seeing as she had an in-country visa, meaning she was there for an extended work period. He noted her passport showed she had left Uganda two weeks earlier and now was back yet leaving again. Sarah had to explain there was a family emergency and she had to leave.

"Why Amsterdam?" the officer asked. "You are traveling under an American passport."

"Oh, my brother lives in Amsterdam and he was taken ill and needed me to look after him"

"Well how ill was he if he needed you to go to him in Amsterdam and yet you were back here in just under two weeks?"

He looked up at her as all African immigration officers do with a cold long stare, perhaps even 10 seconds, which can feel an eternity when you know you're on the wrong side of things. In Africa one of the most powerful positions was to be an immigration officer and it carried the greatest benefits of power. They treated tourists quite differently as foreign currency for the country meant a lot and they had very strict policies from on top regarding the handling of tourists. However, on work visas it was common to cast suspicion ever since the Evangelicals began to infiltrate Uganda.

His lingering stare finally ended, and he stamped her passport. Then Stephen followed her. The officer asked what his business was and why he was in Uganda. Stephen said he was a tourist and came for safari. The officer looked at the passport and then Stephen, and with another shorter pause he stamped the passport. He and Sarah went to the departure gate with a sigh of relief.

# CHAPTER 21
## *The Authorities Await*

They arrived in Amsterdam on time and after clearing immigration and customs, caught a cab to Max's apartment. Max hugged them both simultaneously like a bear. After he let go, Stephen and Sarah noticed Max was not alone but in fact two suits stood behind him.

Max grimaced. "These authorities are from Interpol. They've been waiting for your arrival.

Stephen looked at Sarah and said with his eyes, how did they know I was coming on in on the flight, especially given my forged doc's have passed through with aces up to now? After Stephen introduced himself, he pulled Max aside.

"Did you notify them I was going to be here?"

"No," Max said, "I only contacted Alfred and he told me he'd see to notifying the authorities. Perhaps through Alfred they understood I was the primary contact and accessed my address.

Stephen decided to stay optimistic and let it go. "Well whatever. We're on our way to getting my life back."

The first man from Interpole spoke up. "We'll need to take you to our offices for detainment, but rest assured you'll be released tonight after the first debriefing. We have no need to hold you as we have been in touch with the WHO and understand you'll be working with them." He indicated they needed to get going.

"Can I at the very least take a quick shower after flying through the night for nine hours?"

"Sure but make it quick."

While Stephen was in the shower, Sarah asked Max about getting a cup of coffee. She eyed Max who stepped over to the sink while she was filling the kettle. The suits had moved over to the couch, chatting quietly.

"After Stephen leaves, I'll step into the shower," she said oso the suits could hear. She whispered to Max with their backs to the living room. "Hhow could they have known anything about our arrival?"

"Who knows"'" Max whispered "They just showed up at the door with credentials identifying themselves as Interpol and said they were here to wait for Stephen's arrival. I had no way to reach Alfred as he was in the air traveling to Europe to meet you in Geneva."

Stephen came out of the room not quite fully dressed. He faced the suit who seemed to be the one in charge. "Can I have a minute with my girlfriend before we go?"

The suit said okay, and he and his partner then sat with Max around the kitchen table to have a cup of coffee. Stephen took Sarah for a bit of privacy into the second bedroom to say goodbye for the time being.

"Something is not right," he said. "How did these suits know when I would have been arriving? Only Alfred would have known or perhaps Duvalier from MSF, but we didn't accept Duvalier's helicopter ride as we decided to sneak out of Jinga on the supply plane. There's also something odd about those two guys. It caught my attention when we first arrived."

"What?" she asked. "You're not being paranoid, are you?"

"Their shoes are scuffed and muddy."

"So, what's the big deal?"

111

"Interpol guys are fastidious, Stephen answered, "and regard their stature with great pride."

"Well what do you know. Are you some super spy now?"

"No, but since I've seen every person assassinated who was on my team and the attempt on my life, I have become extremely vigilant, paying close attention to each new circumstance with keen eyes towards everything." He shut down the discussion and asked her to confirm with Max their identification papers. "While I'm finishing up here in the bedroom get Max in private."

"How?"

"Make up an excuse to get him into the other bedroom. Tell him you want to put your things away and ask where you should put them." He then proceeded to finish dressing at a slow pace as Sarah left the room.

She went into the kitchen where Max sat at the kitchen table with the suits. "Max, please show me where I can put away my things as I am sure, based on what the agents have said, Stephen will return this evening and I imagine this will be our house arrest residence until Stephen is arraigned."

When Stephen came fully dressed and out ready to go, as promised, the suits allowed him a few minutes with Sarah to say goodbye. "Well, what did Max think of things," Stephen asked.

"Max said it seemed on the up and up when they showed up at the door. Max had assumed that Alfred via Duvalier and the WHO had set it up."

"No," Stephen said, "I don't like this. Something is wrong. When I leave you and Max immediately go to Max's car and follow wherever they take me. Try to reach Alfred's secretary as he's in the air to see what she knows."

As instructed once Stephen left with the two suits, Max and Sarah quickly hustled down the back staircase to follow. Once in the car, the drove around the alley to the corner and watched Stephen get into the car with the suits. Sarah called Alfred's office on her cell as they drove. Mary answered the phone, but she said she really knew very little other than Alfred caught a plane at 5:30 traveling to Geneva per her reservations.

"She's got nothing," Sarah said. "Let's try to stay close and see if there's anything not quite right or is Stephen just paranoid."

When Stephen had approached the car, the second suit finally spoke, indicating for Stephen to hold out his hands so he could be handcuffed and put into the back seat with a caged separator between the front and the back

"Its standard procedure when we take anyone into a car who is criminally being charged until you are remanded back into custody to whoever is indemnifying your security, which we assume will be your friend Max Brown." As the car pulled away, it was heading outside of the city.

"Why are we leaving Amsterdam?" Stephen asked.

"The Interpol office is in the Hague. Just relax, this will be at least an hour ride."

Max and Sarah were keeping close behind but not too close. Sarah begged him to be careful given the possibility of what Stephen suspected.

"Somethings definitely not right," she said.

"Yes something is afoot here. If they were headed toward Interpol headquarters they would have been headed to the Centrum." Amstel Police Station Max knew well as he was frequently there for further information on stories he was running. The address was 1 Jtunnel 2, 1011 TA Amsterdam. The car the suits were in with Stephen was heading in the opposite going outside of the city.

In the car Stephen sensed his answer was bullshit and started pressing the two suits about where they're really going and who they really were.

The quiet second suit turned to Stephen. "Well I suppose being you're some brilliant bio-geneticist, your entitled to be smarter than most in this situation. Yes, you are right Mr. Kennedy, we are not going to any Interpole agency, as you've obviously have guessed by now. We are headed to meet your former employers. The head of the Group is someone I have been employed with for twenty-five years as head of security. Perhaps you know his name, Heir Dressler? But likely you wouldn't, as the Group always uses intermediaries. It quite common how true leaders of clandestine projects realize the importance of separation between those who plan and those who execute the plan. However, it seems Heir Dressler has now been put into a very difficult situation as the remainder of the group have chosen a different solution, where my Heir Dressler feels there may be a better way out of this. Frankly, that's why you're meeting him today, or else by now you would be dead.

"Heir Dressler and the rest of the Group had hoped their plan would allow the retaking of Africa to reclaim their former property. Their families had conquered and founded Africa. They were the ones who brought it from nothingness and undiscovered vast resources to build a continent of great wealth by developing them—but only then to have them stolen by greedy governments. After the African independence movement that began in the mid-sixties, Africa and its resources have wasted away under their leadership, stealing all the wealth for themselves. So now the Group's plan has failed, due to your interference. We are but the worker bees and we're privy to very little, but we do know you were part of something grand that my employer and his group conceived. Something you ruined.

"So, Mr. Kennedy, we are heading to meet Heir Dressler as he needs to know how far your damage had gone and what the authorities really know, other than the vaccine is toxic. Is the Group really at risk?"

They finally arrived a small farmhouse in a very private area where Heir Dressler's security team had a decent view of the road for approaching cars despite the wooded surroundings.

Heir Fredrich Dressler was the oldest of the Group of Six at age 86, and he was the least prepared to surrender his way of life and wealth. While his other compatriots Fritz Kronner, Franz Heren, Nigel Jones and Roger Atwell believed they would be caught unless they followed their plan of divesting all Africa subsidiaries to protect themselves against exposure by the one person who got away. Regardless of the reality, they thought it best to disappear rather than being captured like Herman Hess, who spent the rest of his life until death in Spandau prison in Berlin.

"Mr. Kennedy," the security head said, "plotting to eradicate millions is not likely to yield anything less than life in prison. Frankly, Heir Dressler is not willing to give up and roll over and disappear until he finds out to what extent you have reverse engineered their plans and identities and given them to the authorities. There's a huge question Heir Dressler has had since you dealt with so many intermediaries. He needs to know who you've reached out to or what they may know. We obviously know you've been in hiding as we have been desperate to find and silence you, but again whether you did or did not speak to anyone or found out anything—those are the questions we need answers to. To your credit you have been elusive, and with the announcement by the WHO, we finally figured you had reached out to someone."

"Since it can't make any difference now," the Suit driving said, "Tell us, where were you? We tried to eliminate you as the others but we failed after cutting the axle on your rental car so you would crash on some country road."

"The accident was the tipoff of your future extermination," the second suit said. "You tripped up the plan, but now the plan has caught up with you.

Max and Sarah were keeping their distance behind Stephen's car. They kept a good distance but sensed these two phony Interpol agents were probably feeling quite confident they pulled off their charade. As they drove Max became well aware that the signs all indicated they were heading towards a small town called Zoetermeer, a vacation spot with small hotels. While they were driving, Sarah was on the phone trying to reach Alfred to tell him what had transpired since they touched down in Amsterdam. Finally, Alfred answered and confirmed there was no way that anyone from Interpol would have known their flight into Amsterdam was arriving that morning.

"In fact," Alfred said, "even I didn't know after I got a call from Duvalier saying you did not catch the helicopter.

"No one knew where you were," Sarah said, "other than Max and I knew thought you were on the way to Amsterdam. However, your secretary said your plans were to fly to Geneva.

"After speaking with Max," Alfred said, "my plan was to make arrangements with Dr. Duvalier who in turn would make arrangements with Dr. Genovese at the WHO so we would all meet in Geneva before we brought this complex situation to the authorities. The plan as I had laid out to Max was, I was going to fly to Amsterdam and we four would fly to Geneva to meet with Dr. Genovese. Perhaps Mary wasn't aware of my last minute flight change. Dr. Duvalier convinced Dr. Genovese that Stephen was an unwitting participant, thinking he was involved in some sort of commercial espionage when he rearranged the DNA sequence. He thought Transgene would test it again to complete the challenge phase with humans. Only Stephen didn't know they had already completed the third phase trail. He thought he was being paid to copy the real vaccine and then rearrange the DNA to ensure the other vaccine wouldn't work. To Dr. Genovese's credit, he understood that without Stephen coming forward through his contact with Dr. Duvalier at MSF, the Transgene vaccine would have been out in distribution already with inoculation starting this week. That it was Stephen who in fact is the sole person who had come to the rescue at his own peril to stop the vaccine distribution and the inoculating of a toxic vaccine which would have spelled death to millions of HIV patients."

Sarah told Alfred that the two phony agents took Stephen in handcuffs and that they were following the car which was not going to the Centrum Police station but pulling into what looked like a small farmhouse. It was isolated by a long road, surrounded by trees for seclusion purposes. She pleaded in a frantic tone with Alfred that he had to reach out to the authorities to get them there as soon as possible, as there was no telling what would transpire in this farmhouse or who was even there.

"Don't worry, I will contact the real authorities immediately." Alfred asked Sarah to pass the phone to Max. "Tell me where you are, what highway, street, house number, postal route, whatever you see by this farmhouse as I'll need it to be explicit for quick action from the authorities."

---

After hanging up the phone, Alfred e paused and considered the most efficient method of action. The Police would require a great deal of explanation and the story was simply be too detailed given the need for a rapid response. With that thought he decided the best bet was Interpol, not the Amsterdam Police, as they were already in a manhunt for Stephen. He googled Interpol and a telephone number came up and he called. A desk clerk answered Netherlands Interpole, how can I direct your call.

"I've got information on the location of Stephen Kennedy," Alfred began, "the Bio Terrorist you've been hunting for, but if you don't act quickly, he could be gone."

"Who are you sir?" the clerk responded. I

"Its unimportant and I'll give you all you need, but you need to get me to someone to act on this immediately."

The clerk transferred the call to the Inspector DeVries who was in charge and Alfred repeated his story, gave him his name and credentials as well as giving him the direct numbers to Dr. Genovese for further credible validation that this was no fake call. He told Devries of Sarah and Max who had trailed the car with those two phony Interpol agents that had taken their "sought after bio-terrorist" to the farmhouse.

DeVries took down the rural route address in Zoetermeer and with dispatch, called around the room for a squad to follow him and off they went to the motor pool and out find Kennedy.

Alfred rang back Sarah and told her what had transpired. The authorities were on their way and likely they'd be there within 30 to 40 minutes. Sarah breathed deep and related it all to Max.

"Don't try to do anything foolish like approaching near to the house," Alfred admonished. "Stay in the car until the authorities arrive. What's most important now is having them get Stephen into their custody. Once he's safe, we will, with the support of the WHO and Dr. Genovese, get Stephen sorted out."

---

As the suits took Stephen out of the car, they kept his cuffs on. They held him at both arms and walked him in. The room they brought him into was a large and well-appointed salon with paintings that seemed to be awfully expensive originals. Stephen had little training with art and other than a Van Goh, Magritte, Renoir, Chagall, and a few others But were he in a market to buy original art, he laughed to himself how easily he could be duped.

The suits sat him at a chair in front of a desk and stood to both sides of him. Still his handcuffs were not released. To his left was a beautiful full hearth fireplace which surely anyone 5'6" could walk into. The walls were stucco with wooden beams and were he not driven there, there could be little doubt he was in a Dutch home.

Within moments an old man, clearly of German descent, shortened over time but likely 6' in his youth. His hair was steel gray and full. His clean shaven features presented a look weathered by time. He sat down as if we were having a business meeting. There wasn't the slightest detection of anger or hostility, but a rather calm demeanor.

He introduced himself with a polite air. "I am Heir Dressler. Mr. Kennedy, there are no secrets between you and me. We both know all of the reasons why we are here today. May I offer you a coffee or tea? As you well know the Orange, that is the Dutch, controlled the South Eastern pacific for centuries and Java was their gold mine bringing spices and tea back to Europe.

"I'd love a cup of tea," Stephen offered, "but surely it would kind of you to first have these handcuffs removed."

"Of course, how rude of me." Dressler proceeded to give Stephen the who story of how this plan was conceived and why it was hatched with the HIV vaccine. "You see Dr. Kennedy, and by the way you have my utmost respect as you are quite the accomplished Bio geneticist, it was in the beginning that our familys built Africa starting in 1660. We discovered with hard work, through numerous generations, this continent's resources and helped supply and build the rest of the western world.

"Imagine now how in the mid-sixties the nations of Africa decided to slough off the weights of colonialism. We who built this continent had to relinquish our holdings to thieves who worked for nothing but felt entitled. The catch phrase, Dr. Kennedy, is entitled. Had they worked or done anything to achieve the prosperity of their nations? No, were we weights upon their shoulders? No. These people were children of their continent and knew nothing of education or development. We colonized Africa and we brought with that improved health standards, education, and civilization. In turn we exercised our rights to take the wealth beneath the continent which was sitting idle and waiting to be developed.

"So, what did we take in comparison to what we brought to the continent? We believe we brought much and built a civilization the natives could not. Well Doctor, now imagine how attractive independence seemed when these new leaders politicized and pressed their people to leave the colonial rulers. Indeed, I can see how they were led down the green path to independence and why people believed that would bring freedom, independence, and wealth.

"Sadly, those who took power were immediately corrupted by the wealth we created. As they say sir, darkness is a sound that is insatiable, and lightness is a call that's hard to hear. Forgive my prose, but this is what happened. The leaders became greedy and only thought for themselves and their families, while they let the common people remain in poverty. Have you travelled to Africa much Dr. Kennedy? Have you been to South Africa with the ANC, Mozambique, Sierra Leone, Mali, DRC, Zimbabw—now that's a true model of absolute greed with Mugabe. However, I mustn't forget that South Africa with its corrupt ANC did pretty well with greed ever since Nelson Mandella's dream died with him. So many successive greedy presidents were put into power by the ANC, like Zuma. And worst of all, those in power simply refused to give it up in places like Kenya, Mali, Uganda, Sierra Leone, Niger—the list could go much further.

"We, our families, our Group of Six as we like to call ourselves, had to relinquish fifty one percent or more of all of our family's holdings as the greedy new leaders insisted. *We* had to maintain operations, but they would control fifty one percent ownership. They call is BEE, Black Economic Empowerment. We see BEE as Black Economic *Entitlement*. The concept is lofty, but where is the recompense for our investment that built what they now have? Well we simply couldn't accept that and seeing as China was taking over Africa via its loan programs, leaving Africa to its own means was a death knell for our assets.

"In any event I digress. Africa needed us and a cleansing, hence our decision to take on this project and soliciting you. But enough of my words. You were brought here as we need to know what the world knows. Please Dr. Kennedy, understand this is not personal. You were the one who answered an advertisement which requested only those people who had nothing in life and no ties. So in some sense you lied to us and now here you are facing the consequences. I do promise you, if you are straight with me, your demise will be quick and painless and all of the money you still hold will be turned over to any family members you designate.

"Is this not fair? Dressler asked rhetorically. "Did we force you to work for us? Who came to whom? but enough of this, time is critical. So, now down to the specifics. How did the WHO find out the vaccine was toxic?" Stephen sat silently. "Come now, its over and we lost. Our plan to cleanse Africa has failed and all we want is to ensure that the authorities cannot trace the plan back to us. Surely you understand that men of power and their families must maintain that power. They who control the purse strings know best how to build the world.

"Well I'm not sure what you want from me," Stephen said. "I never met any of you and only know of Ziffer GMBH and GRC. I only met Brian Smutts who formed the group. I wish I could tell you more but your problem is not with me. I only knew the vaccine was toxic and realized, when I saw all of my compatriots killed, that I was next. On the other hand, what you have, Heir Dressler, is a lot of paper trails from one subsidiary to another, and I have nothing to do with that. I'm only a guy who answered an advertisement seeking a bioengineer for commercial espionage, as Brian told me, or should I say lied to me."

Dressler didn't like his answer but realized this was all too late. Nigel's plan was probably the best. Kennedy seemed like he really didn't know anything, but now he knew Dressler and meant he needed to be dealt with here and now.

Heir Dressler got up. "Regretfully Dr. Kennedy, we do have to dispose of you, but you do have my promise. Your money will be distributed to whomever you wish. Simply give Hans, my trusted associate your information and despite your concerns, your family will receive the money. Now I must go, sir."

In the same breath, on his final syllable, the door to the room burst from a swat style raid. Police bolted in with guns drawn. Hans and his compatriot jumped behind a big stuffed wing back each and drew their guns. Bullets flew from one side of the room to the other. Heir Dressler stood dumbfounded, grabbed his chest, and fell back into his chair. Hans and the other guard kept firing.

DeVries called out, "Drop your weapons! There's no need for this to go further." Hans and his compatriot continued to shoot until his compatriot got hit and fell back.

There was silence for ten seconds which seemed like an eternity to Stephen who had thrown himself onto the floor in front of the desk. Finally, Hans threw his gun out from behind his chair and stood, hands up. The Authorities approached with guns pointed. Hans was handcuffed and taken away.

DeVries reached down to the desk where Stephen was lying. "Well you don't look much like a terrorist, but what do I know is you'll be joining all of us at Interpole in the Hague for now." He picked Stephen up and put handcuffs on him too. DeVries then walked to the desk where Dressler was slumped in his chair. He checked about him for blood and saw nothing. He put his finger to his carotid artery and found there was no pulse. "Don't worry about this one. Looks like the excitement was more than his heart could take. He got off easy. We'll get a morgue truck out here to take him and the other one lying on the floor in. In the meantime, take these two back to HQ, however make sure you keep the bio terrorist in a separate car, as I'm not sure what's going on here, but there's no doubt he's in a different class from this henchman."

As they exited the farmhouse Stephen came into view and Sarah ran to him. At first the two policemen pushed her away but then DeVries called to them. "Give them a moment together. Whatever the hell is going on here, its these two people who alerted us," he said pointing to Max and Sarah, "as to what was transpiring and were waiting for us."

# CHAPTER 22
## *The Plotters Story Unfolds*

At the Interpol station, Hans was put into a block where violent criminals were kept. Max and Sarah sat in an integration room with DeVries. They explained as much as possible and truth be told, DeVries was having a hard time believing any of it until Dr. Duvalier arrived from Schiphol airport just 20 minutes after they had sat down.

Duvalier had phoned the Police Centrum after letting Sarah know he had arrived and was on his was over. He asked Sarah to put Devries on the phone. Upon confirmation of all of the story details, DeVries finally understood that Kennedy was not a bioterrorist but an out of work, unlucky idiot, by way of a false solicitation, and was brought in as an unwitting participant in what he thought was simply a case of commercial espionage. DeVries finally understood from Duvalier that in fact by Stephen in coming into the light, he will save millions of lives, even if he was part of the genesis of it all.

When all was said and done after almost 90 minutes, DeVries agreed to permit Stephen to be remanded into the custody of Dr. Duvalier from the MSF and allowed all of them to go to Max's apartment. He agreed to have a special team of police pick them up at the apartment the next morning to catch a flight to Geneva. DeVries had already contacted the real Interpol, as the Amsterdam Police had no jurisdiction other than giving the four of them up to an Interpol agent when they arrived at Schiphol Airport the next morning to take their flight.

After the four left the Police Centrum, DeVries called the Interpol offices in the Hague to make further arrangements for special security, getting the most senior level officers to the airport to escort them to Geneva. They would have no jurisdiction limitations anywhere within the EU. DeVries wanted to prevent any interceptions by those still at large who might try to stop them from reaching Switzerland.

The next morning DeVries would turn Hans over to Interpol for interrogation. At the Police station, the one thing now very clear to DeVries was that Hans would be helpful in getting the other criminals involved in the plot to assassinate millions with a toxic vaccine. Hans was fingerprinted and quartered off to a cell.

When Stephen and company left the station in a police van, it was driven by two of DeVries best officers. The four entered the apartment and they collapsed between the sofa and chairs.

After a few minutes, Alfred said, "I've got a room at the Krasnapolsky hote. It's a favourite old landmark of mine. So, I think I'll catch a cab and head over there to get settled. I think I've had enough excitement for the day and probably its best we meet at the airport in the morning."

As Alfred got up to leave, Stephen offered to walk him downstairs. "There are no words to convey my feelings," he said. "After not having seen each other in all these years, you rallied to assist me and believed in me. Without you, I'd still be on the run. You should be lauded by the authorities as much as anyone for saving millions of lives and preventing this toxic vaccine from seeing the light of day."

"No, you're the hero bro!" Alfred said. "Your life was the one on the line as they hunted you while the world ganged up labeling you a bioterrorist. Despite what fate might have awaited you, you were willing to risk it all, possible assignation and now prison to save those millions of people. I always knew you were the soul of a man with integrity. Despite the incredulity when you told me the story, bonds built by former roommates of nearly a decade together are strong! When you live day in and day out with someone as the years go by, you really get to know who they are at the core. Once you said that you were innocent and were being hunted, I knew no matter what was being said about you, it couldn't have been true." Alfred's arm went up and as several taxis were passing by, one saw and immediately stopped. As Alfred was getting in, he turned back. "Relax guy, this is all going to be alright."

Stephen returned to sit with Max and Sarah. They were each exhausted.

After a minute of silence, Max said, "It's been a hell of a day. To say I never experienced it's like before or believed it possible would be an understatement. How about we each take a couple of stiff vodka shots!" They did, and after about 30 minutes, Max spoke up again. "I don't know about any of you guys, but I'm starving."

"Oh yeah, me too," Stephen said.

"There's a sweet little Rijsttafel nearby. We don't even need to look at menus. We'll have a great spread of Indonesian cuisine."

After dinner, as they entered the apartment, they bid each other good night with Max into his room while Sarah and Stephen went to theirs.

"Until tomorrow," Max said, "when we will all travel to Geneva, make it a good night you two love birds, you've earned it!"

Sarah and Stephen dropped onto the bed, side by side and stared into each other's eyes. Stephen suggested a shower, but Sarah reached over and grabbed his face and began to kiss him gently. She moved her lips from his face to his wrists, red from the handcuffs. In a few minutes, Stephen began pulling Sarah's dress down and she began unbuttoning his shirt. Slowly as they caressed each other, Stephen pushed Sarah down and gently slid upon her body while softly pushing her legs apart. Their love making was slow at first but became frantic until they both climaxed.

They laid side by side until falling into a deep sleep. Sarah dozed off first. Stephen lingered a bit despite his exhaustion, but finally gave in to showering in the morning.

Alfred arrived by 8:30 the next morning. Max, Sarah and Stephen readied to meet two senior security Interpol agents. It was clear everyone was on edge as to what this day would bring for Stephen. The arriving agents were security, not tactical. Interpol agents carried different ranks based on the work being handled. The two meeting everyone were Level III security agents.

Interpol agents ranked from I to III in tenure with their two different departments, Security and Tactical Operations. The two who rang the apartment to fetch them were the highest ranking in security operations. They drove the van to a side entrance gate at the airport leading directly onto the tarmac. A small, private jet operated by Interpol awaited. It was a short 90-minute flight to Geneva. When they arrived, they were met by another Interpol security detail to escort them to Dr. Genovese at the WHO offices. When they arrived, all were escorted to Genovese's office where two additional Interpol tactical level III agents waited. These were the personnel who were leading the criminal investigation.

The now eight plus Dr. Genovese all adjourned to a conference room with extra sound insulation to try to keep things as secure as possible. It was an active investigation, and they wanted no prying eyes or ears. Ordinarily this type of investigation would be conducted at the Interpol headquarters in Brussels, which was the seat of Law Enforcement for the European Union. However, as the literal technical aspects of this vaccine resided at the WHO in Geneva, top security and tactical decided it was best to have all parties there to expedite the investigation.

The meeting began with questions from the senior tactical agent. His name was Detective Lucas Goossens. He was chosen to lead the tactical team as he was Flemish, one of the two primary languages spoken in Brussels but for those who resided in an Arab district. Brussels had a large Arab contingent, and Arabic was spoken commonly by the numerous former residents of the north African Colonies that migrated to Brussels since the sixties and seventies as more of these counties sought independence.

French and Flemish, which is closest to Dutch, were the primary languages spoken in Belgium. Headquarters decided as Goossens was Flemish by the home he was raised in, he was the best tactical candidate as Transgene was South African. Many in South Africa spoke Afrikaans, which was very close to DutchI. In Geneva, French was the primary language used in the offices and laboratories, although English, in the past 30 years, had become a requirement for all of those employed at the WHO as a second language.

"Stephen, to try to recap how he became involved in this crime," Detective Goossens asked.

Alfred objected immediately. "Let's refrain from implying that Stephen was a criminal."

"I apologize.s Dr. Kennedy was only complicit by ignorance. Nevertheless, I need everyone to work with me and not take anything personally."

Stephen chimed in, "Please go on Detective. I do not take the word 'crime' or 'criminal' personally. Whether I was aware or not, the crime took place and it almost cost millions of lives in Africa and I accept the implication."

"Okay," Goossens continued. "How were you solicited into this crime?"

Stephen began at the very beginning going back to 2008. "At that time, I had lost my job after the crash, when all of the big pharma took a huge hit. It seemed as far as Wall Street went, the sky had fallen. The loss of my position and its accompanying salary put my life and marriage in peril. At first the bills piled up, and then the foreclosure of our house. I suppose I was extremely depressed and began to drink heavily. Upon reflection, I'm sure it had a negative impact on my wife, which contributed to her affair with some guy from work. We never had children due to an issue with her fertility. While she wanted to adopt, I refused, thinking as a geneticist we could overcome this with some new in vitro fertilization procedures. She had been working in a law office as a clerk and well—"

Goossens interrupted. "Listen, I regret your personal tragedies, but we need to get to this case, not your personal life that led up to this crime."

"I'm sorry. It seems every time I come to this intersection of my life and how it all spiraled out of control, I'm reminded of what drove me to answer that advertisement. In any event with my marriage gone, I was quite forlorn and began seeking something to take me away from my current empty life. I went onto the web looking into worldwide trade journals and entered a search for foreign overseas opportunities in Biotech. I found this advert which said, 'must have an advanced degree in Biotechnology, preferably a PhD, single, without ties or family, seeking a clandestine biogenetics opportunity in a commercial venture, with a very large payout upon a successful completion. Travel to Africa will require a 3-month stay. All interested parties should write to ziffer@ziffer.GMBH."

"I never heard anything further from Ziffer, but within two weeks a phone interview took place with a Brian Smutts from a company in South Africa called GRC, which was short for Genetics Research Corporation, Ltd. I was sent an email with e-tickets to Zulu Natal, South Africa's third largest city. I was met by Brian Smutts. was put up in a hotel, and the next morning we had breakfast along with four other individuals who all had expertise in more military ways. I'd be glad to give all of their names, but regretfully you'll find they're all dead.

"After we were paid out to the tune of 1.5 million, as the weeks went by, after we—I, cloned the vaccine and redesigned the existing DNA in a process I thought was simply making it inactive, I saw through various news outlets the names of my compatriots who had died in strange accidents. I knew then these weren't coincidences. They had all been eliminated over a three to four week period. Only then did I realized what I was involved in was not just commercial espionage. I reconsidered all of my notes and it dawned upon me that I was a dupe, an idiot who actually rearranged the DNA to create a toxic vaccine at body temperature. I had inserted a new gene using a specialized restriction enzyme which cleaved a part of the genetic code into a delayed toxic immune response.

"We had spent three months together preparing for the break-in to Transgene, and we all got to know each other quite well. Much about our sad histories was shared at evening dinners. Inevitably, when you're living and working in this type of circle, while waiting for D-day, the moment of truth, we often spoke about what we would do with our monies and where we would go. The first fellow eliminated I found out about on a evening news. They said it was a road accident.

"A week later I saw something in a newspaper about a computer genius from Sweden making a quick rise in prominence with a tech company. Yet it was cut short with a tragic hit and run accident on High Street in Stockholm. When I learned of the first two deaths, I tried to track down the third on the team, only to learn from his family that he had disappeared. They had no idea where he was. I knew he had said was going back to school at Witswaterrand University in Johannesburg. I checked at the University and they had no record of him.

"With their deaths I knew I would likely be next. The money we were all paid by whomever was behind this plan meant nothing to the payors. It was comparatively inconsequential compared to their plan to eradicate tens of millions in Africa and reclaim their assets and prizes."

Goossens broke in. "Where did you come to this information about what these individuals who hired you really wanted? Did they tell you?"

"No," Stephen responded. "I didn't need to once I realized what I had done. Beyond that I learned from Heir Dressler before I was rescued by the Amsterdam police. It filled in all the missing pieces I might still have had in my head. He told me I wasn't going to be leaving our meeting alive, but if I cooperated, my death would be quick and all of my money would be distributed to any family or anyone I would wanted. He wanted to know how the WHO found out the vaccine was toxic and who else I had been involved with. Basically, he wanted to know who knew what. Believe me, at this point my pants were brown. Alfred, Sarah and Max looked at each other with incredulity. Had it not been for Max and Sarah reaching out to Alfred who got DeVries to the farmhouse, I've no doubt I would be dead by now."

"Did you ever learn much about Brian Smutts, your initial contact?"

"A little," Stephen answered, "but he, aside from my four other teammates, is now dead. Obviously, everything and everyone was to disappear as part of whoever put this plan together."

Goossens told the group that Devries had gotten the fingerprints processed on the older fellow who died of a heart attack when DeVries team stormed in. "His name was Fredrick Dressler. He was a former member of the Nazi party although he never served as an SS officer. He comes from a very old German family and it seems he and associates calling themselves the 'Group of Six' were all part of this clandestine operation. The deviousness of their plan was that the formula you inserted into the DNA sequence had an undetectable flaw. As we learned from Dr. Genovese the vaccine only became toxic when it went into humans where body temperature would change the nucleus inside CD4 cells, depleting them at an accelerated rate." Goossens turned to Genovese. "Did I get that right?"

Genovese chimed in for the first time. "Quite perfectly. It had the opposite of building CD4 cells to create greater immunity. I must admit you are a quick study to have absorbed all that from our phone conversation."

"The authorities realize you were duped into this," Goossens said. "But reaching out to Alfred and eventually Dr. Genovese, you became a hero in saving millions when you could have stayed in hiding with your 1.5 million dollars."

"Thanks for the flattery," Stephen replied, "but once I realized what I was complicit in doing, it wasn't about being a hero. Genocide can never be permitted in our world again. No matter the risk, I had to do whatever was in my power to stop it. Whether they killed me, or I went to prison, either was preferable to knowingly participating in such inhuman catastrophe on a scale exceeding anything Hitler had tried to do during WWII."

Sarah turned to Max. "So just in case you're wondering why I fell in love with this guy…" They all smiled.

"How did you learn about these people who refer to themselves as the Group of Six?" Stephen asked.

Goossens explained that DeVries had this fellow Hans Gierter, who was captured in your rescue, and has been under interrogation by the at Police Centrum in Amsterdam. "He gave us Heir Dressler's name and explained his 25 years as head security officer. It seems his loyalty became quite translucent once he realized what his former boss and associates were involved in. The idea of even remotely being connected to the death penalty loosened his tongue very quickly."

"What's next with this Group of Six?" Stephen asked.

"We will pursue them. Not a rock in Europe will remain un-turned. We know about Ziffer GMBH and its clients and subsidiaries. Interpol has good corporate and accounting forensics. There is always a trail to be followed. With Dressler dead, the other five will be found and brought to justice. The crime of genocide is one from which no one escapes, at least if we've learned anything from WWII. As for you Stephen, your heroics have earned you a probationary term of 5 years, and you must agree to assisting Interpol in whatever manner we deem necessary."

Stephen's eyes of relief met Sarah's. No jail time would be forthcoming, and they would be able to resume life together, living and loving and having that family they both wanted.

Goossens gave an ahem, as Sarah and Stephen's gaze lasted several seconds. "I don't think there's much more to be done here. I was hoping to get more from you but it's clear they kept you in the dark, however we would like to get from you the names of those on your team who died. We believe that while there is little that can be done for those dead, we will be able to get the criminals who were responsible for their deaths beyond the Group of Six. It may also, in turn create additional leads. Those following orders to murder need to be cleansed from the cities of Europe.

# CHAPTER 23
# *Death and Diaspora of the Six*

Nigel, upon getting news of Dressler's death via his contacts with the Amsterdam police, was shaken to the core. It was confounding. He had tried to explain during their last meeting that the only way out was to dissolve all African assets and become a little poorer. He had believed everyone was with the program. However, it seemed that the old man, Heir Dressler, had his own options to pursue before he would relinquish his assets. The idea that the only way out of their situation was the divestiture of their holdings, eliminating any trail back to the Group must have been repugnant to the arrogant old man. He had escaped prosecution during WWII as a Nazi SS party member, stealing millions in artwork from the Jews. He must have felt untouchable. A pity. Seems he was as greedy as our African derelicts.

After that somber consideration, he grabbed a bourbon off the bar, and took a moment to contemplate the next best next move. He decided everyone needed to be alerted, at least as a courtesy, but he saw himself and Roger Atwell as separate entities within the Group of Six. Roger and he went to school at Eton, grew up together and were at least a decade younger than the rest of the group, being in their mid-sixties.

After the Groups's last meeting to discuss the failure and where they would all go, Roger and Nigel returned to England and had a private meeting of their own. They both agreed it was beyond the necessity of divestiture. What they needed was an escape plan to a country where there wasn't extradition to western nations. Roger proffered they needed to find an island somewhere, the Maldives perhaps.

"No, money is always the route of corruption," Nigel replied. "We must find a locale where most of the corrupt world keeps their assets. A country isolated from threats by wealthier nations. The Maldives may be remote, but they have no money and hence they are at the whim of larger nations. I suggest Panama. I'm a bit surprised it didn't occur to you, but then again, you're a solicitor not an accountant. As a chartered accountant I know many of our wealthy British compatriots hide their paper assets, such as Bearer bonds and other types of financial instruments, there."

Nigel went on to explain how Panama had become a country of choice for accountants to hide money. The nation had been doing it so long that their wealth was more than 40% tied to foreign hidden money and financial assets. The laws were beyond liberal because if the country became subject to retrieval of assets and funds, the nation would go bankrupt and the economy would be devastated.

"It's not a commodity rich country," Nigel said. "When Trujillo overthrew the government in 1968, Noriega was head henchman and that was the beginning of Panama's hands-off policies that allow corporations to hide their money there."

Nigel and Roger agreed, putting aside any further discussions of divestiture, that their immediate destination, until life for them returned to normal, would be Panama.

Nigel relaxed a bit after a stiff double and told Roger he had no doubt that their time was very short. He asked about where in the process the legal paperwork was to eradicate any trails back to them.

"It's in progress, but I'm not sure it all had been completed," Roger answered.

Nigel continued in deep frustration of the calamity before them and further explained that Dressler got a few of his corrupt Interpol contacts to pick up Kennedy. Dressler took it upon himself to kidnap Kennedy and invent his own plan. His paid goons used their credentials to capture Kennedy and take him to a remote location outside of Amsterdam where he still owned a farmhouse. It went sideways as the police somehow got word of where Kennedy was and sprang into action.

"But how did they know where to go?" Roger asked.

"Someone tipped off the Amsterdam police," Nigel said. "It appears wherever Kennedy was staying, when these two corrupt Interpole goons picked him up, his friends became suspicious. They followed them to the farmhouse, then tipped off the police who wasted no time, given who they thought Kennedy was to capture him."

"How did you get all of this information?"

Nigel smiled. "I, too, have my sources. The rest of the story leaves little more to be said. When the Police got there, a short gun fight ensued as Dressler only took his prime bodyguard Hans Gierter and another guy to avoid any of us knowing what he was planning. Geirter was captured and is in police custody. The other one is dead, and Dressler died there of a heart attack. We need to alert Franz Heren, Fritz Kronner and Roger Collier to tell them it's time to initiate the retreat plans they set for themselves. It's every man for themselves until enough time passes to dissolve the connections between the Six. Nigel told Roger to get all assets wired to Panama and gave him the bank instructions.

"Get yourself on a plane to Panama City. Check into the Intercontinental and I'll meet you there."

---

It had been ten days Goossens met with everyone at the WHO in Geneva. On the eleventh day, he made arrangements for Franz Heren, Fritz Kronner and Roger Collier to be picked up by Interpol agents.

They were taken in handcuffs to awaiting vans for transport to Brussels for arraignment. They would be eventuallybe sent to the Hague to stand before the World Court for Prosecution of their heinous crimes.

During the time since Stephen had provided the information regarding Ziffer and GRC, Interpol had done its forensics work and had found direct connections to all of the Six. Ho doubts remained. Even with the dissolution of assets and holdings in Africa, the timeline couldn't be dismissed. It was all too quick.

It was amazing, however, that when Interpol agents interviewed each presidential leader from various African countries where the members of the Six held assets, not a one claimed they had any knowledge of them, despite newly swollen bank and brokerage accounts. but the missing pieces of the two youngest of the Six still mystified him. Nigel Jones and Roger Atwell, who both had a pedigree going back to Eton, were elusive. Roger the attorney and Nigel the accountant, were nowhere to be found. It was as if they had disappeared off the face of the earth.

Within six months, trials were held, defense lawyers presented their arguments and the prosecution presented overwhelming evidence. The court found Heren, Kronner and Collier all guilty and sentenced to hang for crimes against humanity. In the end, the defense presented a powerful argument against the death penalty. They cited the plotters' ages and that the crime was never committed. Yes, the plot was heinousness, but ultimately unsuccessful, causing no direct loss of life. The Court of International Justice decided, given such a defense, to countermand the death sentence and instead institute life in prison, for whatever time they had left.

# EPILOGUE

Within a few years after the case was closed, a new HIV vaccine emerged thanks to the work of Stephen Kennedy. Stephen had become a prestigious researcher at the WHO and worked directly under Dr. Genovese. For all concerned, from Goossens to Devries, life resumed its normal flow. Stephen Kennedy and Sarah were eventually married and had the children they talked about and lived a wonderful life in Geneva, Switzerland. Alfred returned to Wall Street and saw his company come to fruition cloning organs for intra-uteri babies. Max won a Pulitzer Prize for his story on the HIV vaccine plot to kill millions. The article was titled "The Cure."

Goossens went on to a directorship at Interpol for solving and bringing to prosecution those involved in the plot. However, he was always confounded regarding the two that escaped, Nigel Jones and Roger Atwell. The mystery haunted him for several years until finally one day in April 2016, he opened a copy of the London's Herald Tribune to read an article disclosing of one of the world's largest money frauds ever uncovered in Panama. The story came to be known as "The Panama Papers."

The article began with the list of names of those indicted, and there it was. Two of the names listed were Nigel Jones and Roger Atwell. A smile formed on Goossens face.